Any d
was

Bolan's foray into enemy territory was no longer soft probe. He was going to have to fight his way out if he wanted to stay in the game.

Picking up the sound of raised voices close by, he heard the scrape of boots on concrete and figured there were two, three guards at the most. He flattened himself against the front wall of the house, the big Desert Eagle leveled and ready.

His guess had been correct. Three armed men came into sight, bunched close as they cleared the building. Bolan let them step into full view before he opened fire.

The Desert Eagle thundered in the close confines. Bolan emptied the magazine, his calculated shots on track, sending the trio of would-be shooters down in a bloody tangle.

Bolan jammed his weapon back into the holster and freed the 93-R. He needed to maintain his pace, not give the opposition any opportunity to gather themselves. His sudden appearance had already disturbed their equilibrium.

The Executioner had to keep up the mood.

MACK BOLAN ®
The Executioner

The Executioner
Don Pendleton's ®
HOSTILE FORCE

A GOLD EAGLE BOOK FROM
WORLDWIDE ®

TORONTO • NEW YORK • LONDON
AMSTERDAM • PARIS • SYDNEY • HAMBURG
STOCKHOLM • ATHENS • TOKYO • MILAN
MADRID • WARSAW • BUDAPEST • AUCKLAND

Recycling programs
for this product may
not exist in your area.

First edition January 2013

ISBN-13: 978-0-373-64410-0

Special thanks and acknowledgment to
Mike Linaker for his contribution to this work.

HOSTILE FORCE

Printed in U.S.A.

Do all the good you can. By all the means you can. In all the ways you can. In all the places you can. At all the times you can. To all the people you can. As long as ever you can.

> —John Wesley
> Founder of Methodism
> 1703—1791

By my efforts I will wage my War Everlasting, dedicated to those who have been, and who are being, delivered pain and suffering by those who profit from misery. They walk upright. They talk with human voices. But they will never, ever *be* human and are to be denied pity. And until my last breath I will seek them out and crush them into the earth.

> —Mack Bolan

THE
MACK BOLAN
LEGEND

Nothing less than a war could have fashioned the destiny of the man called Mack Bolan. Bolan earned the Executioner title in the jungle hell of Vietnam.

But this soldier also wore another name—Sergeant Mercy. He was so tagged because of the compassion he showed to wounded comrades-in-arms and Vietnamese civilians.

Mack Bolan's second tour of duty ended prematurely when he was given emergency leave to return home and bury his family, victims of the Mob. Then he declared a one-man war against the Mafia.

He confronted the Families head-on from coast to coast, and soon a hope of victory began to appear. But Bolan had broken society's every rule. That same society started gunning for this elusive warrior—to no avail.

So Bolan was offered amnesty to work within the system against terrorism. This time, as an employee of Uncle Sam, Bolan became Colonel John Phoenix. With a command center at Stony Man Farm in Virginia, he and his new allies—Able Team and Phoenix Force—waged relentless war on a new adversary: the KGB.

But when his one true love, April Rose, died at the hands of the Soviet terror machine, Bolan severed all ties with Establishment authority.

Now, after a lengthy lone-wolf struggle and much soul-searching, the Executioner has agreed to enter an "arm's-length" alliance with his government once more, reserving the right to pursue personal missions in his Everlasting War.

1

Mack Bolan had never been one to shrug off his responsibilities. His commitment to those he had shared experiences with in the past remained firm. When Bolan picked up a familiar name in a dossier the Stony Man Farm computer team had downloaded, he delved into the report and his suspicions took form and developed into a deep concern.

A combined U.S./U.K./European operation, an investigation into Organized Crime run by the customs services of the concerned countries, had been compromised. Somewhere within the agencies involved there was a leak. As the operation was targeting international OrgCrime with criminal conspiracies, the interagency involvement was ripe for problems.

Two men were already dead—an American agent and his German counterpart. One more man had gone missing.

It was the missing agent's name that drew Bolan's attention.

Ethan Sorin, U.K. Customs and Excise.

Mack Bolan had Sorin as a short-term partner during a previous mission. Sorin had been wounded during the course of the investigation. Bolan recalled the man as a good ally in that short time.

Bolan understood the problems the agencies were having, because he understood how OrgCrime worked. It was the modern-day equivalent of the old-time Mafia—high-level criminal activity for high profit. Nothing was sacred. If it brought in profit and increased the overall power of the criminals, they would work it to the limit. Bolan also knew there was only one way to deal with the hyenas: go for the throat. Do it to them first and do not let up until the head is severed from the body.

As Bolan read the dossier, the more he became aware of the reach of the criminals. The interagency group had uncovered some of the OrgCrime involvement: human trafficking, drug and weapon trading, stolen-car rackets and prostitution on a wide scale. With some of their dealings being closely scrutinized, the OrgCrime mob had used its influence and insider knowledge to block investigations. Violence and intimidation. Bribery. These people used any method necessary to protect their business.

With the killings and the disappearance of an agency agent, the interagency force found itself at an impasse. Until they could source the leak, they couldn't make any important decisions for fear that they might be intercepted.

Bolan's interest was heightened by the problem and the missing agent. He could not ignore the details about Ethan Sorin. The Brit's background detailed his return to the U.K. following the mission with Bolan and his transfer to U.K. Customs. There was also mention of the fact that although both his parents were dead he had a sister.

Sorin had been injured on that mission with Bolan because he had sided with the American, and, Bolan being Bolan, he couldn't distance himself from that. He had no deep-seated guilt, just an acceptance of responsibility.

Bolan asked Kurtzman to gather all the data he could on the IA—the interagency—its people and background, and also known associates within the OrgCrime group. He asked Brognola to fix him up with a flight to London and to supply him with any contacts the Fed could locate.

"You could upset a lot of people if you step into this," Hal Brognola had said.

"I hope so," the Executioner replied.

"I'm not talking about just the perps."

"Neither am I, Hal. Two agents are dead. They deserve something to be done."

"And Sorin?" Brognola asked.

"And Sorin," Bolan said. "He helped me out once. Took bullets that could have killed him. Now he needs help."

Brognola sighed. He understood. Mack Bolan carried a big serving of loyalty for those he called friends. Nothing he waved around like a banner, just a quiet truth he exposed from time to time. No fuss. No fanfare. Just the essence of the man. It was the reason others saw him as someone they could naturally trust.

The other side of the coin was the Executioner. The man who stood against injustice. Against true evil. The man who faced his enemies and brought them down with the cold efficiency of the warrior he was.

"Okay, Mack," Brognola said. "We'll be here if you need us."

Bolan smiled. "Hell, I know that."

2

Greg Henning, former antiterrorist operative, had worked on a mission with David McCarter, the Phoenix Force commander, getting himself wounded in the process. His injuries had compromised his ability to perform with his old unit so he had been transferred to the U.K. Customs Service. Henning was philosophical about the move. In his own words, he was still fighting the bad guys.

"Jack said to send you his best," Bolan said.

Jack Coyle was one of McCarter's cover names.

"He called to say you'd be in touch," Henning said. "With Jack's past record I know you haven't called to ask for a charity donation."

Bolan smiled, trying to imagine McCarter's description of him.

"Are we safe to talk?"

"Now I know you're a friend of Jack's. And yes, this is a secure burn phone. No one listening in and no record of the call."

"Ethan Sorin. Any idea where he is? Or if he's still alive?"

"You don't waste time," Henning said.

"My people picked up background on your problems. Told me all I needed to know."

"I know about his injury. It's why he was sent back to the U.K." Henning gave a dry chuckle. "Last time Jack was here and I got pulled into his case I ended up in hospital, too.

What is it with you blokes? Does everyone who works with you get shot?"

"Not all the time," Bolan said. "You were working terrorism then. Now you're on the OrgCrime beat."

"A career change," Henning said. "What can I say."

Bolan didn't pursue the matter.

"If you're up to speed," Henning said, "you have as much information as we do. Two of Sorin's team were executed. Can't call it anything else. The bullets were recovered and matched to other killings linked to the mob. But that's all we can be certain of. Now Sorin's disappeared and he hasn't been in touch since. You may have read that we seem to have someone in the agency passing along information?"

"We worked that out."

"Sorin was in the know. Which is most likely why he won't make direct contact. Just before his disappearance he sent a message to say his team had got their hands on data that would go a long way toward breaking the mob. He was going to bring it in. Next thing we knew his team had been hot and Sorin had dropped out of sight."

"You've got a rotten apple in the barrel."

Henning sighed, a sound of frustration and resignation.

"Same happened with my last assignment. It was why I got myself shot. On my own doorstep. Bastard was waiting for me. And here we are again. Another son of a bitch selling us out. What do you think? Am I lucky, or what?"

"Greg, you do what you can with the cards you're dealt. Don't beat yourself up about it."

"Okay, self-pity over. What can I do for you, Cooper?" he asked, using Bolan's cover name.

"I'm dealing myself in for Ethan and your agency. If you can help, fine. If it goes against your principles I can respect that, too."

"If you can do something about these buggers you have my vote. What do you need?"

"I want to start cutting into the mob's dealings. Show them

they can be hurt. Won't be the first time I've come up against these people. The only way to get their notice is to hit them where they'll feel it."

"One of our problems is we can't swing into action at a moment's notice. Takes organizing. Maybe this is where you can move without waiting."

"I'm listening."

"I have a source. He's been feeding me information for a few years. Always genuine. He came to me yesterday and offered me a tip about the mob bringing in a container of merchandise from Europe."

"What kind of merchandise?" Bolan asked.

"The live kind," Henning said. "Human-trafficking. One of the mob's more lucrative sidelines."

Bolan had experienced this vile trade before. Captured human beings were sold into virtual slavery to be used and abused in various ways: prostitution, illegal labor, pornography. Drugged and beaten and subjugated. The poor wretches were treated like cattle by their own kind.

"Will your guy deal with me?" Bolan asked.

"He will if I tell him to. And pay him."

"Greg, set it up. I'll meet your man and he can deliver me to the drop. Let's make these bastards stand up to be counted."

HENNING'S INFORMANT was a forty-year-old named Joey Ballantine. A lean, hungry-eyed man with a nervous disposition and a battered, paint-faded Jaguar saloon. The car might have looked ancient but its mechanics were in top condition. A little like Ballantine. Despite his bedraggled appearance the man was sharp and didn't miss a trick.

"Nice bloke, Mr. Henning," he said as he drove Bolan out of London and onto the route that would take them to their destination. "Treats me right. Always pays on the dot and he looks after me if I have any problems. Upset me when I heard he'd been shot that one time. Pretty close thing, too. But he pulled out of it. He's a hard man, but fair. When my sister's boy got himself into trouble with the law it was Mr. Henning who got it all sorted. Even helped get the lad a job. Yeah, he's a great bloke."

Bolan made no comment. He simply sat and watched the scenery flashing by. He had no idea where they were now, London had disappeared a while ago. He read a few road signs, but none meant much to him.

Ballantine had picked him up a few hundred yards down the street from Bolan's hotel. The man had then answered Bolan's questions about the container with sharp, to-the-point replies.

"You're certain about everything?"

Ballantine nodded, not offended by Bolan's inquiry. "I always double-check my sources, Mr. Cooper. If I slip up and pass along bad information it isn't going to be helpful to anyone. I lose my credibility, I'm finished. And the wrong people, yourself included, might get hurt. Can't have that."

They arrived at their destination with time to spare. Ballantine pulled the Jaguar to a stop. They were on the coast, in an area that had a desolate, empty look to it. Abandoned industrial buildings led to the water's edge. Tall, rusting cranes stood in acres of cracked, weed-sprouting concrete littered with detritus.

A sudden squall of rain hit them, coming in off the sea. Steady and chilled, it suited Bolan's mood.

"Years ago this used to be a busy dock. Never as big as some others, but it paid its way. Now it's only used by small freight companies as a facility for container traffic." Ballantine smiled. "A lot of illegal stuff finds its way through along this part of the coast."

They stepped out of the Jaguar.

Under his long topcoat Bolan was clad in his blacksuit. It had brought a brief moment of interest from Ballantine but nothing else. Henning had told him to deliver Bolan to the site and not to ask questions. Bolan's ordnance was in a backpack.

"See where the containers are stacked," Ballantine said, pointing beyond the sagging wire-link fence. "Three long storage warehouses next to them. Dock Two is where the ship will be moored. She's called *The Wanderer*. That's where a container will be craned onto a trailer and hauled away. I didn't get where the delivery point is. My source wasn't able to find out."

"No problem, Joey. I'll take it from here."

"You want me to stick around, Mr. Cooper?"

"Thanks, no. You get back to town."

Ballantine opened his door. "You put my number in your phone?"

Slipping off his topcoat and dropping it on the passenger seat, Bolan nodded. "If I need anything else I'll call."

The Jaguar turned around and left.

Bolan picked up his backpack and slipped through the fence.

He had a rendezvous to keep.

3

Bolan took a long, circuitous route to the dock, using the rusting piles of machinery for cover. He had almost reached his destination when he spotted a patrolling heavy, sporting a squat SMG. The guard was wearing a wraparound weatherproof coat to protect him from the rain, and a sodden ball cap was pulled down across his eyes. He moved slowly, with grudging reluctance at being delegated to tramping around the site. Bolan waited until the man moved past his position, then slid unseen into the shadows and closed in on his target.

The ship moored against the crumbling concrete dock was a tired-looking freighter. Rust streaks showed on the scraped paint of the hull. Bolan picked up the name stenciled on the bow, confirming it was the one Ballantine had spoken about. As Bolan hunkered down between stacked oil drums he was just in time to see a steel shipping container being swung by crane off the deck of the freighter and moved in the direction of a waiting tractor-trailer combo. The container would be placed on the flatbed of the trailer and locked into position.

Bolan waited as the container was loaded. The freighter crew, including the roving guard, turned and made their way back to the comfort of the dry ship, leaving the operator of the transporter to fasten down the clamps and secure his cargo.

Turning, Bolan edged his way to where other steel containers formed a line along the edge of the dock exit road. A plan was forming in his mind as he climbed up onto the containers and waited for the truck to move off.

He needed to be at the rendezvous point when the truck arrived with its illegal cargo. The pickup crew was his target. Bolan did not want to miss his chance at striking at them.

There was no option left. The rig was leaving. He knew what he needed to do, and, as risky as it might be, Bolan saw no other way. If he was going to follow through, he needed to act *now*.

He pulled a pair of black leather gloves from his pack before he slipped his arms through the straps, securing it across his back. He watched the container rig easing away from the dock, moving along the quayside. Its course for the exit would take it along the line of stacked containers, and Bolan knew that they offered the opportunity to make his move. He began to work his way across the rain-slicked tops of the containers, moving quickly as the rig began to pick up a little more speed. A swift glance ahead showed that the line of containers ended in about a hundred yards. Bolan had to strike fast— and not miss his step. One faulty move and he could easily slip. Bolan registered the notion and immediately dismissed it. He did not live his life on regrets.

The rig was some four feet below his level, the top of the container glistening with rain. Bolan powered forward, moving until he was close to the front of the rocking surface. He needed to allow himself some leeway. There was a three-foot gap between the rig and the stacked containers.

The end of the stacks was coming up. Bolan pushed forward, knowing he had to take the jump. He veered to the edge of the container, arching his body forward, pushed off and seemed to hang in midair for an eternity before he dropped.

His booted feet struck the wet surface, but lost their grip on contact. Bolan felt himself drifting to the far edge of the moving surface as the rig bounced across a pothole. One leg cleared the edge of the container. Bolan threw out a gloved hand, his fingers grasping at a metal lifting ring. His other leg stretched out, his foot finding a lodging point against one of the cross struts. For a moment his body gave in to the shift of the container, then he managed to pull his free leg back onto the flat surface. He twisted away from the edge, splayed out across the roof of the container, and lay motionless.

Bolan felt the container move as the rig took the turn out of the yard. The container might have been secured to the trailer base but it still swayed as the vehicle turned. He braced himself, gripping the metal lifting ring, feeling his body slide again. Bolan wedged his boots against the cross struts. He had no idea how long his journey might take so he would have to put up with any discomfort.

Twenty minutes into Bolan's ride the rain increased. Being on top of the container meant he was fully exposed to the chill downpour. Within a couple of minutes he was completely soaked. Coming in from the North Sea, the rain was cold. Luckily, his body-hugging blacksuit was able to withstand the downpour and the gloves he wore prevented his hands from becoming frozen. Bolan's face was exposed and his skin tingled from the rain striking it. His thick hair became plastered to his skull. David McCarter often explained that the reason the U.K. was so green was because of the everlasting rain. Bolan realized that the Brit had never been joking. Every word he spoke was proving to be true.

The rig followed the coast for the most part, not moving inland until almost an hour had passed. Widely distanced, isolated farms showed up occasionally. Then there was a long stretch of uninhabited terrain before the rig slowed and made a right-hand turn. It bumped its way along a rutted, partly overgrown concrete road. Derelict buildings were visible in the pale light. The placing and construction of the structures, with the wide spread of flat land extending beyond, told Bolan they were on one of the long-abandoned Second World War airfields found in this part of the country. From these sites British and American aircraft had taken off for forays into

Europe, delivering their payloads of deadly bombs onto German cities and factories.

The rig rolled beyond the smaller buildings until the humped shapes of the old aircraft hangars came into sight. From his vantage point Bolan saw a number of vehicles parked near one of the hangars—three panel trucks, and a pair of high-end SUVs. He counted at least seven men in a loose group waiting by the vehicles. They all wore heavy coats against the rain.

As the truck drew closer Bolan saw that three of the waiting men were carrying SMGs.

The rig slowed, then stopped. Bolan slid to the center of the container's roof, away from the edge where any movement might be spotted. He eased the backpack from his shoulders, opened it and took out his combat harness, shrugging it on and securing it. He checked the Berretta 93-R in the holster. Then he drew out the Uzi that was nestling inside the pack. He retrieved three loaded magazines and located them in pockets on his harness. He repeated the process with extra magazines for the 93-R. A couple of smoke grenades and an M-34 phosphorous grenade hung from his harness.

Bolan heard the sounds of the container locks being freed, the doors being dragged open. They were swung wide to bang against the container's sides.

"Okay, let's move, you lot." The harsh command was accompanied by someone banging on the side of the container with something metallic. "Come on, come on, we don't have all fucking day. Get your skinny arses out of there before I come in and kick you out."

Bolan hung the Uzi round his neck and reached down to his harness, closing his fingers over the smooth cylinders of the smoke canisters. He held the levers down as he pulled the pins, then slid to the side of the container, looking down at the parked vehicles and the group of waiting men. They were just starting to move to the rear of the container. Bolan let go of the levers on the canisters, lobbing them down into the straggle of men.

Despite the rain the thick coils of white smoked began to hamper the figures. The sudden disturbance had a disruptive effect on the group. Bolan rose to a crouch, Beretta in hand, moving quickly to the rear of the container. Below him, the man who had opened the doors was still yelling at the human cargo that clustered at the edge of the container. Bolan knew that at any second the smoke would become visible and he would register what was happening.

The guy reached out and caught the sleeve of a hesitant girl, yanking her viciously from the container. The girl screamed, stumbling as she slammed to the ground, falling facedown.

"Hey," Bolan said.

The guy looked up, his eyes widening as he saw the dark shape of the Beretta in Bolan's hand. The 93-R spat out a single, suppressed 9 mm slug. It made a neat hole in his forehead and a significantly larger one as it blew out the back of his skull. As the man fell, Bolan holstered the Beretta, grabbed his pack and slid over the edge of the container, hanging by his hands for a couple of seconds before dropping into the body of the box. He unloaded his backpack and immediately brought the Uzi into play. The human cargo shrank back from his black-clad form, unsure what to make of his sudden appearance.

"Stay back," Bolan commanded. He gestured for them to retreat, then dropped from the bed of the container to the concrete. He stepped over the body of the man he had just shot, turning to face the reception committee.

The first guy to show was one of the armed men, emerging from the coiling smoke, his angry face glistening from the falling rain. Whatever he might have been expecting, an armed man dressed in a black outfit was obviously not on his list.

"Who the bloody hell are..."

He failed to complete his question. He also failed to bring his SMG online. Bolan triggered the Uzi, hitting the man with a burst of 9 mm slugs that turned him from living to dead in a matter of seconds. The short burst drove into his chest and ravaged his heart. The man uttered a brief cry, fell backward and hit the wet concrete with a solid thump.

Bolan dropped to a crouch, ducking beneath the overhang of the container and worked his way close to the double set of rear wheels. He leaned out and opened up with the Uzi, laying down hard bursts of fire into the scattering figures still partly enveloped in the thick smoke from the canisters he had launched.

In between the crackle of his weapon came screams and moans, and not a little wild yelling and cursing. Bolan closed his ears to the din. He was not concerned with the suffering of the traffickers. They had forfeited their rights when they embarked on their chosen path. The rights of their victims had already been violated—the Executioner was simply delivering the justice those victims could not. The Uzi clicked on an empty magazine. With the ease instilled in Bolan by his use of the weapon, he dropped the used mag and slid a fresh one in its place. Bolan resumed his rapid fire, driving the opposition away from the container rig and back to the grouped vehicles.

Bolan gave the traffickers no breathing space as he crouch-walked to the opposite side of the rig, emerging upright and making his swift way along the vehicle. He skirted the tractor unit and came into the open behind the scattering traffickers. The thick smoke was dissipating quickly, exposing the panicked group. They were seemingly leaderless, each man shouting orders that were being ignored, and increasing the rising fear that was rendering them unable to make coherent decisions.

Bolan's swift glance took in the bodies already on the ground. Some moving, others still.

A tall, hard-faced man, brandishing a handgun he didn't seem capable of using, had turned and was heading in Bolan's direction. He didn't spot Bolan's dark figure until the last moment. His face, already fairly pale, lost the final vestiges of color as he saw the Executioner. Given his startled appearance he suddenly remembered he was holding a weapon. He yanked his arm around and pushed the autopistol in Bolan's direction.

"Bastard," he yelled in a moment of pure defiance.

It was his final word.

Bolan's Uzi crackled—a short, effective burst that dissolved the guy's face into a bloody, shattered mask. The man buckled at the knees, folding forward, blood spouting from his head and soaking the front of his expensive topcoat.

In the time it took for the man to hit the ground, Bolan plucked the M-34 phosphorous grenade from his combat harness, while sending a burst of 9 mm fire at the window of the closest SUV. The glass shattered. Bolan pulled the pin of the grenade and tossed it through the shattered window of the vehicle. He pulled back and heard the grenade detonate. The thermal grenade threw out its fearsome power, the released phosphorous swelling to 5000°F. The generated heat destroyed the SUV's interior, blew out all the windows and ignited the gas tank. The resulting explosion threw blazing fuel out in a fiery ball that slammed against the side of the steel container, rocking it against the clamps holding it in place.

Dazed, with clothing scorched and burning, the surviving traffickers staggered away from the blazing wreck, their resistance subdued by the overall effects of Bolan's intense strike. They had no idea what had just happened—nothing like this had ever occurred before. They had always believed the mob was protected. Invulnerable.

But the unthinkable had happened, and they were out of their comfort zone.

None of them knew they had just been subjected to a Bolan Blitz.

A concentrated strike by the Executioner.

Bolan reversed direction and moved to the open rear of the container again. The people inside, protected by the steel shell were confused and scared. Like the traffickers, they had no idea what had just happened. Their bewildered faces peered out at Bolan. He shrugged his pack over one shoulder.

"Anyone understand and speak English?"

"I do."

The voice came from the girl who had been dragged from the container and dumped on the ground. She had a darkening bruise down one side of her face but seemed unharmed otherwise.

"Tell them they will be safe now," Bolan said. "Get them out of the container and over there." He indicated the open ground away from the container. "Keep them together for the moment until I can settle things here."

The girl nodded. She began to issue orders in a firm tone, urging the women and girls to leave the container. She called out to Bolan after speaking to one of the women.

"Two are dead. There are others who need attention."

"I'll deal with it."

Bolan turned his attention to the traffickers, his Uzi covering the sorry-looking group. Out of the seven he had counted, only two were still on their feet.

"All weapons on the ground now," Bolan ordered. "Don't give me an excuse to put you down." His Uzi stayed on the men while they did as instructed. "Now move away and stand against the front of the hangar."

"What about them?" one of the traffickers asked, indicating the wounded on the ground.

"Take them with you."

"They need medical attention, you bastard."

"You expecting sympathy? Maybe we should ask your passengers. Somehow I can't see them being too willing to extend you any, either. Especially the ones who are dead."

When he had the traffickers assembled Bolan ordered them to throw down their cell phones, too. Then he moved back, keeping them under his gun as he used his own phone to make contact with Henning.

"Don't you ever think some people might need a break?"

"Greg, you sound cranky. Did I wake you?"

"Very funny."

Bolan gave Henning a quick rundown on recent events. The Brit listened, heaving a heartfelt sigh when Bolan told him about the dead and sick victims.

"Where are you?"

"About an hour and a half from where Joey dropped me off. The container rig I hitched a ride on ran east along the coast road, then turned inland after an hour. We ended up at an old wartime airfield. I firebombed one of the vehicles, so it should show the cops the way in."

"We'll get a chopper in the air. They'll find the place and guide the ground teams in."

"Greg, get your people here ASAP. I need to move on. Keep the mob on its toes."

"Without the rule book of course?"

"Your so-called rule book is pinning you guys down so you can't move in any direction. There's bad blood somewhere in your setup, feeding the mob on every move you make. Flush him or her out. If you don't, you'll not only lose more of your people, but also your ability to mount effective operations."

"You know what annoys me most?"

"What?"

"That you're bloody right, Cooper. I'll have the local cops move in and take over. Medical teams, as well. I suggest you head out the minute you hear them coming."

"Thanks, Greg."

"I'll wait ten minutes before I make the call. Can you be clear by then?"

"I'm already gone."

Bolan ended the call. He located the English-speaking girl and told her what was about to happen. He ordered the traffickers to move their wounded into the container, then made them climb inside. Bolan slammed the container doors shut and secured the locking bars.

"They won't be able to get out of there," he said.

The girl nodded. She threw her arms around Bolan and gave him a hug.

"Thank you. From us all."

"You'll be looked after," Bolan said. "I have to go."

"Are you not with the authorities?"

Bolan smiled. "Not in the way you might think," he said.

The girl watched him commandeer the remaining SUV. It had been sitting away from the other vehicles so it hadn't suffered any damage when the firebombed vehicle had blown. He placed his backpack in the truck as well as the cell phones he had taken from the traffickers. He eased out of his combat rig and pushed it into the pack along with the Uzi. Bolan powered up and drove off the old airfield, turning the SUV toward the north.

He had been driving for almost a half hour when he heard the distant sound of sirens. He pulled onto a narrow side road and into the cover of trees and bushes and waited until the convoy of police cruisers and ambulances had sped by. Then he rejoined the main road and kept driving. His cell rang twenty minutes later. It was Henning.

"I just had a call from the cop heading the task force. They're well pleased with what they found at the airfield, but they can't figure out the way it went down. Only one of the victims who speaks English says they heard arguing before the shooting and believe it must have been some kind of gang fallout."

"It can happen, Greg. People like those traffickers are pretty unstable."

"The girl is giving chapter and verse about where they were snatched. Descriptions. Some locations, though she can't be too clear on those because for a lot of the time they were kept locked up."

"If you get ID on any of those traffickers…" Bolan said.

"I'll pass on what I can," Henning said.

"Grateful."

"Where next? Or shouldn't I ask?"

"Better you don't," Bolan said, then ended the call.

A small town loomed in of the distance. Bolan drove slowly along the single main street until he spotted a clothing store. The window display showed mainly agricultural wear, which suited Bolan's needs. He parked the SUV and went into the store. The man behind the counter studied him carefully, taking in the black outfit.

"Had my jacket stolen earlier," Bolan said. "I need a waterproof coat."

"Rack just to your right," the man said, pointing.

Bolan checked the displayed garments. He tried on a loose-fitting waxed garment. It felt right. Bolan took out his wallet and handed over his credit card. As they completed the transaction the man behind the counter nodded toward the SUV.

"Good-looking motor," he said. "Looks like the latest model."

"Yeah. Nice ride."

"They come with everything fitted now. Even built in SatNavs. You got one in there?"

Bolan smiled. "Wouldn't be at all surprised," he said.

Back in the SUV, Bolan ran a check on the cell phones he had confiscated. He didn't find anything helpful until the contact lists kept coming up with a common name. Bolan called Joey Ballantine and quoted him the name.

"Mean anything to you?" Bolan asked.

"Yeah. Heard it before. Don Lawrence is the *man* in London. He runs local operations for the mob. Well-protected. Henning's tried to catch him a few times but Lawrence is a slippery bugger. He's lawyered up to the neck. Can't be touched."

"That's about to change," Bolan said.

"How did your visit to the docks go?"

"A satisfactory result. Do you have a location for Lawrence?"

4

"Who the hell are you? I don't know you."

"Right now, Lawrence, I'm a very important man in your life. In fact, I'm the only one who matters."

Don Lawrence stared at Bolan. He sat upright, moving his shoulders casually, and a degree of confidence returned.

"If you know so much about me you'll understand not to mess about. Our organization doesn't respond to threats. We have ways of dealing with them." Lawrence managed a cocky smile. "Be careful what you say."

There was a subtle change in Bolan's expression. It was enough to make Lawrence hold back his next remark. The blue eyes of the man staring at him took on a chill intensity that matched the tone of his voice.

"Larry Cobb was found dead in his car outside his Paris hotel. Bullet through the back of his skull. The same as Ernst Schiller, except he was left in a ditch outside Munich. The slugs removed from them matched. Came from the same weapon."

"What does that have to do with me?"

"It has to do with the fact that the gun in question has been linked to a number of murders your mob had a hand in."

"You can prove nothing, even if it might be true."

"We both know it's the truth, so don't play games with me. I'm sure you've heard by now about the delivery point at the airfield. You lost men and a cargo. That was only the start.

I'm here to pass on a message. Make sure your people hear it. You've run your string. No more free passes. I'm going to cut your mob apart. Take you down piece by piece. The minute I walk out that door you're all targets. No bargaining. No exceptions. From bottom to top. Bagman to head honcho. It's all over, Lawrence. Put out the word. Accept the fact you are *all* walking dead men."

The 93-R moved, the muzzle centering on Lawrence's face. It held there for a time and Lawrence began to sweat. The beads ran down and stung his eyes. He tried to blink them away. He ran his sleeve across his eyes and when his vision cleared and he could see again the black-clad figure had gone.

Lawrence heard the click of the apartment door closing. He reached and grasped the Glock autopistol holstered under his jacket, gripping it hard. He didn't pull it from the holster because he could feel his hand shaking.

The big man in black had scared him. No doubt there. He might not reveal that fear to anyone, but the man had been scary. Something in his manner. His voice. And those icy blue eyes. Whoever he was, the guy had been in earnest. It had been no idle threat—no hollow words. He had meant what he said. Lawrence was convinced about that. His actions at the airfield had shown he was not fooling around.

He didn't know how or when or where, but the man dressed in black was going to cause problems for the mob. That was a certainty.

Lawrence understood something else. The man was no cop. He was no OrgCrime agent, either. Okay, his accent was American—he hadn't made any attempt to hide that fact. But he had made direct threats against the organization. And Lawrence was in no doubt he would act on those threats.

He glanced across the room to where Lex lay. His minder had been a good companion. A brutal, psychotic individual who had little respect for anyone in his way. The man in black had put him down without hesitation when Lex had gone for him. He'd avoided Lex's attack, his powerful hands snapping the man's neck as easily as breaking a bread stick. The act had defined the man's skill. It wasn't a big move to imagine those skills encompassing the organization.

Lawrence picked up his cell phone, hit a speed-dial number and waited for his call to be picked up.

He had a message to deliver.

He was not looking forward to it.

"Don, you sound agitated. What's wrong?"

"I'll tell you what's wrong. I just had a visit from some bloke dressed all in black who told me to pass on the fact he's going to close us down. He was the same guy who hit the airfield drop-off."

"What the hell do you mean he's going to close us down?"

"Just that. Shut down the organization. Tear us apart. He said to tell you we are all walking dead men."

There was a long pause. Then a cold laugh.

"Who was this fuck? This has to be someone's joke of the month, Don."

"*Really?* I'll tell you who isn't laughing, Corrigan. Lex isn't laughing because he's lying on my bloody floor dead. My visitor snapped his neck when Lex tried to throw him out."

The silence this time ran on for a while.

"This doesn't make any sense, Don. No sense at all. No one screws with us."

"Well, this guy was serious. You should have been here, Corrigan. He was tooled up. I thought he was going to shoot me."

"Not a cop? One of the OrgCrime team?"

"No, I don't think so. But he knew about Schiller and Cobb. Said the slugs they pulled out of them matched. And he said he had proof the gun had been used in other related killings."

"What about an accent? Where was he from?"

"He's American. Big feller. Over six feet. Black hair. Bloody cruel blue eyes."

Corrigan said, "He familiar at all?"

"Not to me. Corrigan, you should beef up security. That's

your job, isn't it? Whoever this bloke is he's got good intel. He knew about the cargo pickup. He found out where I live. And he has facts we can't ignore."

Corrigan grunted his assent. "If he was out to make a point he did just that. We'll have to scratch the airfield. Can't use it again. But we need to keep up with our deliveries. Check your lists, Don. You have commitments to keep. Frasko will be wanting to move another shipment. We need to be ready with a fresh delivery location. Work on it, then call me soon as you have it ready."

"I'll speak to Markel and have him arrange a video conference for the heads. They need to know what's happened and what this bloody American said."

"Good luck with that," Corrigan said.

"Cheeky sod," Lawrence said. "Last thing I need is that bugger Frasko throwing his weight about."

5

Rene Markel was having a difficult time holding back his impatience. He hated video-conferencing. He much preferred face-to-face meetings. However, that was one of the drawbacks of long-distance dealings. The way the mob was set up there were few alternative methods to bring everyone together. Leaning back in his seat he picked up his pack of French *Gitanes Brunes* cigarettes and lit one with the heavy gold lighter he always carried. The strong tobacco gave him a brief lift and he gazed around the conference room, eyes taking in the expansive view of the city beyond the soundproof glass of the wall-to-wall window. In the hazy distance he could see Notre Dame. He never tired of the view. Paris was his city. He loved it with a passion. Every brick. Every street and alley. Its smell and color. The restless mood that inhabited the place. Sun or rain, it made no difference. If he had been forced to make a choice, Paris in the rain would have been it. Streets glistening. The very smell of the city freshened by the persistent drizzle. People rushing for cover. Markel drew on the cigarette, a wistful smile curling his lips.

The computer made a beeping noise as the final participant came online. Don Lawrence from London. His face on the large monitor looked strained, dark bags under his eyes. For once he had forgone his pristine appearance. He looked harassed.

His image did not go unnoticed by the others on the video link.

Lec Frasko from Albania.

Hans Coblenz, who was calling from Hamburg.

From Italy, Marcello Astrianni.

And from the U.S.A., the head of the east-coast group, Anthony "Tony" Lowell. He was also, by default, the boss of the bosses.

This was the first time they had been brought together in an emergency meeting for a long time. They spoke on many occasions in one-on-one conversations, and their subordinates were constantly in meetings relating to business. But for the heads of the groups to speak en masse was a special moment.

"We all know why we're here," Markel began.

He spoke in English as it was a language known to them all, and it saved time and the chance of mistakes if they had to work through translators.

"Don," Lowell interrupted, "what the hell is going on over there? Sorry to jump in, Rene, but this is too important to worry about fucking niceties."

Lowell was well known for his lack of diplomacy. He had grown up on the streets, having had to fight for everything he wanted and the experience had left him with little time for polite conversation.

"We had an incident at the pickup point in the east of England," Lawrence said.

Frasko leaned forward, his grim features twisted into an angry scowl. "An *incident*. You lost valuable cargo," he yelled. "Twenty-five pieces of merchandise I had transported to the U.K. without a problem. And you lost them."

"You think I did it for fun?" Lawrence countered. "I lost men. Some dead, others arrested. We were hit by some trigger-happy shit who came out of nowhere."

"Hah," Frasko said. "You had enough men there and one took them down. What kind of idiots do you employ?"

"You think your Albanian arseholes could have done better?"

Frasko thrust his face close to the screen. "My grandmother could have done a better job."

"From what I hear she does her best work on her back," Lawrence said.

"Enough," Lowell thundered. "We're here to work this out, not call each other names. Now cool it down. If we can't iron this out between ourselves then we are quickly going to end up in a mess." He cleared his throat, taking a drink from a tall glass of iced water. "Don, for the benefit of those who haven't heard, repeat what this guy laid out for you."

Lawrence, as they all knew, was the point man in London. He was the organizer, the money man and the guy who hired and fired.

"In brief this Yank paid a visit to my apartment after the airfield hit. He killed Lex. Snapped his neck right in front of me. He made it clear he was responsible for the airfield hit. His message, for us all, was to say he was going to put us out of business. The organization would be ripped apart and *we* are all his targets. Walking dead men were his actual words."

Coblenz said, "Shouldn't we be considering *who* this man is? Yes, he has information the OrgCrime force knows about. But he does not operate like any agent I have ever heard of."

"Hans has a valid point," Lowell said. "This guy comes out of nowhere and carves up our people like a loose cannon. Okay, the OrgCrime squads are bound to be pissed off because we dropped a couple of their agents. But those assholes don't take a leak without checking the orders of the day, and they do not send out some independent shooter. Their legal people would be having collective heart attacks if they even raised the question."

"So are we looking at some rival mob?" Astrianni asked in his heavily accented English. He stroked a hand through his thick black hair, a nervous habit he had. "Is this going to become a war?"

"No way," Lowell said. "Who would have the balls to stand up to us? No one. Jesus, let's not start getting paranoid. Look at the facts. One guy comes in, takes down Don's crew, and next thing the cops are crawling all over creation. This screwball wasn't looking to take over the cargo. He lets the cops take 'em."

"What then?" Lawrence said. "Is this bastard a vigilante or something? A do-gooder trying to clean up the streets?"

"An independent operator," Markel said. "Could be a black-ops deal. Brought in by government."

"Which government?" Frasko said.

"What about an outside contractor?" Lawrence said. "Like the private-security companies working in Iraq and Afghanistan?"

"That's possible," Lowell agreed. "Some of those ex-military guys will go the extra mile if the money is good."

"It does not matter who," Coblenz barked, his voice ringing with Teutonic sternness. "We need to do something before it happens again. We need to protect ourselves."

"We all have businesses to maintain," Lowell said. "None of us have the time to handle this personally, so we need to bring in *our* man. Give him the facts and turn him loose."

Markel smiled. The Frenchman knew exactly who Lowell was referring to. He had used the mob's troubleshooter himself.

"Corrigan," he said quietly. "Yes. Give it to Corrigan. Let him pick up the scent and hunt down this bastard."

NO ONE RAISED any objections. They were all familiar with Lowell's man. He had never failed to bring any assignment to a satisfactory conclusion.

His latest operation had resulted in the termination of the OrgCrime agents—Schiller and Cobb.

Both of them, closing in on the European division of the group, had been efficiently taken care of by the man. Corrigan had been furnished with the names of the agents, their locations delivered to him by the mole within the OrgCrime ranks, and had completed the assignment within a week.

Unfortunately a third agent, a Brit named Sorin, had vanished. Even Corrigan had been unable to locate him. He was still looking. Lowell would make contact with Corrigan and bring him up to speed with the current situation. He would add the search for the rogue American to Corrigan's list. Point him in the direction of the interloper. Sorin would still be looked for by one of Corrigan's additional teams.

"Leave this with me," Lowell said. "This is why we have Corrigan on standby. He'll bring his boys on board and hunt down this son of a bitch."

"Tell him to make it quick," Frasko said. "We can't have any more fuck-ups. Business will begin to suffer if this American is not hunted down."

The Albanian was a hard man who had no time for anything that interfered with business. His intolerance was a trait no one liked, even the other heads of the mob. He challenged everything and everyone. Frasko was indifferent to his business partners' dislike of him. They had to put up with it because he was good at his job. His snatch teams were the most proficient, gathering up young women and girls from the streets and delivering them where requested. The incident at the airfield had been the first example of anything going wrong. It was hardly Frasko's fault, but he would use the moment to express his impression that other parts of the mob were not operating efficiently.

"Okay, okay," Lowell said. "Leave the arrangements to me. Corrigan will be on the case by the end of the day. Right now we need to move on to other business. Marcello, you wanted to talk about the distribution of that consignment of narcotics...."

6

Corrigan could never recall when he had acquired the title of "the Cleaner." It had been around for such a long time, it neither interested nor bothered him. He only thought about it briefly when the name was bandied about by others.

The Cleaner.

In moments of quiet reflection he accepted that it did sum up his purpose. He did clean up the messes created by others, but that was as far as he dwelled on the matter.

He was more interested in the moment. And, as he broke the connection with Tony Lowell after receiving his new orders, his mind was already assessing the challenge of the mission ahead.

In essence it was a simple enough order. Locate and eliminate the unknown American who had interrupted delivery of a cargo, taking down most of the crew and placing the valuable merchandise in the hands of the police. There were also the details of the man's visit to Don Lawrence and the killing of Lex, the bodyguard. As far as Corrigan's personal feelings were concerned Lex had forfeited his life because he had not been good enough to take the guy. A simple enough fact.

He pushed to his feet and sauntered across the apartment, staring out through the window at a rainswept London. Dark clouds scudded in, fragmented by the strong breeze. He might have seemed to be simply observing the weather. In truth, his mind was already working on what needed doing.

He turned and crossed to the wet bar. He reached for the cigar box resting on the black onyx surface and removed a long Cuban. He bit off the end with strong white teeth, lit the cigar with a silver Zippo and savored the tobacco.

Corrigan was tall, close to six-five. He kept himself in shape with regular exercise. Not out of vanity but with a need to be in good condition. He was three years off forty. Good-looking without being handsome, with regular features. His hair, thick and brushed straight back, was dark, a few gray strands beginning to show at the edges. His eyes, a dark shade of blue, looked on the world with caution. He had little trust for anyone or anything. His abiding confidence in his own abilities was the only thing he believed in.

That confidence had kept him alive and at the top of his profession for the past fifteen years. In that time he had only ever made one real mistake in judgment. On an early mission his carelessness had cost him. And the third finger of his left hand had been the price he paid. Since that day he had never once allowed anything to stand in his way. He had never dropped his guard again. And he had never failed. Exactly one week after the incident all those years ago, with his hand still bandaged, Corrigan had finally caught up with his adversary. His retribution had been swift and had served as a warning to anyone else who might stand against him. The rival enforcer had been rolled out of a car and left lying in the gutter following his brief disappearance. He was minus all ten fingers.

Corrigan brushed a flake of ash from the front of his dark blue Sea Island cotton shirt. He favored expensive clothing because he could afford it and also because he liked to appear smart. His size meant he often found it difficult to find what he wanted on regular clothing racks, so he only went to the best. He used outfitters in London and New York and Paris. Just as he had apartments in all three cities. His work for the mob meant he travelled extensively. He didn't like hotels, preferring his own surroundings. His regular crew travelled with him, permanently on call. It saved time, and he always had his group on his wavelength so there was never any need for extensive explanations when a mission came up.

He would call them in presently, using a single-use cell on a party link so there was no chance of anyone tracing his call. His team used similar status phones, an unlimited supply of the cells being available from one of their suppliers. Corrigan put the phone on Speaker as it rang out and he waited for his team to come online.

Four of them. Hard, experienced operatives who understood his needs and did as they were told without exception. They had all come from the streets. Though they were rough and undisciplined when Corrigan had recruited them from the lower ranks of the mob, he had trained them, tutoring them in the ways of the profession. If Corrigan had pride in anything it was in his crew.

Pikey and Lapdog were both from London. Lean and wiry, with that ever-hungry look of the street. A deadly pair of soldiers who had learned the only man they could trust was Corrigan.

Delbert was a solid African-American man from New York. His quiet demeanor was simple cover for a savage in expensive clothing.

Markus came from Serbia. He had once been a combat soldier; his skills were broad-reaching and his loyalty to Corrigan unwavering.

Corrigan's call was answered quickly.

"Change in plans," Corrigan said. "We have an additional assignment on top of Sorin." Corrigan paused. "Any ideas what it might be?"

"Anything to do with that hit on the pickup crew at the airfield?" Lapdog volunteered.

"Good thinking that, man. Exactly right. We go after him. Identify him and make him go away."

Markus said, "As in dead?"

"If we can take him alive we do. But if the bastard wants to play hero, put him down hard."

"He's only one mother," Delbert said.

"Listen up, all of you. Do not play this guy down. He's serious competition. Took on the pickup crew and cut them to pieces. You all knew Lex. No beginner. This guy snapped his neck as easy as that. What does that tell us?"

"That he's no cherry," Delbert said, admonished.

"We don't know who he represents?" Markus asked. "Or where he came from?"

"Could he be part of a covert team?" Pikey said. "I mean, could there be others?"

Corrigan shrugged. "You guys tell me. It's what we need to know. This is what you're trained to do. Go out and do some checking."

No one asked *where*. Corrigan expected his team to work with self-motivation, to use the skills he had embedded in them. He would be watching and assessing whatever they came up with, coordinating their results and making final decisions.

"Check in regularly," he said. "Keep each other in the loop. Decide where each of you wants to go and use all the resources we have available."

Markus said, "I'll check the docks. See if anyone remembers anything."

"He took one of the pickup crew's SUVs from the airfield. I can get details and see if I can track it. SatNav might give me something." This was from Lapdog.

"We'll get on it," Markus said.

Delbert was left on his own after the others had spoken. Corrigan sensed the man had more to say.

"Del?"

"This guy already has information," he finally said. "Knows about those OrgCrime agents. Maybe he figures that Sorin dude might have something that could help him."

"Right," Corrigan said. "We already know that. Which is why we need to find Sorin. So what are you thinking?"

"Let the others concentrate on the guy. Like you said, Sorin is keeping low on the radar, but we still need to keep him in our sights. Let me spend some time following through."

"Okay. What do you have in mind?"

"Sorin has family. Could be worth looking there. It might be Sorin has made contact, even if it was just to let them know he's alive. It's a long shot. If it don't come to anything, we write the family off."

Corrigan nodded. "Go with it," he said. "I'm going to check our assets. This guy interests me. He's real, so maybe *somebody* knows something about him."

7

The county of Buckinghamshire, around forty miles from London, was a world away from the frenetic inner-city noise of the capitol. Driving along tree-lined roads that wound between small, quiet villages, seeing large houses standing back in their own grounds, Bolan immersed himself in the tranquil beauty.

Henning had furnished Bolan with coordinates he fed into his SatNav and the gentle Irish voice of the guide directed him to the gates of Clair Sorin's home.

Bolan had abandoned the vehicle he had commandeered at the airfield when he had reached the city. There was always the chance it might be tracked so he'd left it behind, dumping it and walking away, calling Joey Ballantine for a ride back to his hotel. Henning's informant had obliged without complaint, becoming even happier when Bolan had handed him a wad of banknotes from his backpack reserve. He had dropped Bolan outside the hotel.

"They must have you on a bloody good expenses rate," Ballantine said when he eyed the five-star accommodation.

Inside, the girl on the desk smiled at Bolan as he asked for his room keycard.

"Back late, Mr. Cooper," she said.

"All-night poker game," Bolan said. "Win some, lose some."

"How did you do?"

Bolan said, "Tonight I held the winning hand."

After a sound night's sleep Bolan dressed, ate breakfast, then took the elevator down to the basement garage where his rented SUV was parked. His holdall went with him, stowed in the back of the vehicle. He keyed in the address for Clair Sorin and drove into the hectic snarl of London traffic.

Three years younger than her brother, Ethan, Clair was a widow in her early thirties. Her husband had been a successful investment banker with his own company in the city. He had collapsed and died from an unexpected and massive heart attack. At the time, Clair was running a riding stable on the grounds of the family home and had continued to devote her time and energy to the investment business. But a year after her husband's death Clair had sold the investment business to one of the partners—it had left her an independent and wealthy young woman.

Henning's detailed information had told Bolan that Clair was extremely close to her brother. Neither of their parents was still alive, so the two of them were all the family each had.

It was thin information, but for Bolan it was a starting point. Enough to prompt him to make a house call.

The SatNav informed him he was within a mile of the property. Glancing out the window Bolan saw white fencing bordering the estate. He slowed, his gaze checking out the surrounding landscape. On either side of the road, deep grass verges, dotted with trees, added to the rural atmosphere.

Bolan's Irish guide's charming tones told him he had a quarter mile to go.

Bolan caught a fleeting glimpse of something off the road just ahead, on the left. He didn't turn his head, simply allowed his eyes to move as he drove by.

A large, high-end SUV, dark blue, tinted windows. Then he was by and continued on his course. The image of the SUV was fixed in his mind.

The SatNav informed him to turn right after two hundred yards and that he would then have reached his destination.

Up ahead he caught a glimpse of dark red roof tiles. The

big house was set back from the entrance. The white wooden gates stood open and Bolan turned up the wide, gravel drive and followed it through a short avenue of trees and bushes. The drive widened into a generous oval at the front of the house. To the right, away from the house were the stables. A mix of red brick and wood, the stalls were fitted with Dutch doors. A number of horses' heads were visible over the lower sections of the doors. Bolan rolled to a stop near the house and climbed out.

He presently wore civilian gear. Tan slacks and a dark shirt under a sport jacket, and a pair of strong leather shoes. The jacket was loose enough to conceal the shoulder rig holding the Beretta 93-R.

Bolan saw the front door was open, showing the wide, polished-wood floor of the hall that appeared to run the width of the house. He was moving toward it when the sound of horse hooves on hard stone caught his attention. He turned and walked in the direction of the stable, clearing the end of the house. A wide yard, stone-cobbled, fronted the L-shaped stable building.

A tall, handsome chestnut mare stood motionless as its rider slid easily from the saddle. The rider was a woman, above average height, thick blonde hair falling free as the riding hat was removed. The woman shook her head, loosening the mass of hair. Her shapely, lithe figure was well-defined by a snug-fitting roll-neck sweater and cream jodhpurs. Knee-high leather riding boots completed the ensemble.

Bolan took one look at her and knew she was Ethan Sorin's sister. The likeness was startling, though Clair's features held a feminine softness. When she turned to look in his direction, Bolan recognized the color of her eyes and the firm line of her mouth.

"Can I help?" she asked. Her voice was steady, well-modulated. A slim girl appeared from the stable to take control of the horse. "Jane, give her a rubdown and a little water once she cools." She returned her attention to Bolan, smiling easily. "Sorry about that."

"No problem," Bolan said. "It's you I've come to see, not the horses."

"Oh?" she turned her head slightly, scrutinizing him closely. Not entirely suspicious. More cautious. "You're not selling anything, are you?"

Bolan shook his head, smiling easily. "No. I've come to talk to you about Ethan."

He had her full attention. Clair hesitated for a few seconds, then said, "Do you know my brother?"

"I was involved in something and Ethan helped me out."

"My brother the hero." She grinned.

"My name is Cooper—Matt Cooper," Bolan said.

Clair ran strong fingers through her hair. "I think we should go inside, Mr. Cooper. Would you like a cup of coffee? If I say so myself, I make good coffee." She smiled disarmingly. "Being American you'll be able to confirm or deny that claim."

She led him back to the house and inside, her riding boots clicking against the smooth wooden floor. They went all the way down toward the back of the house, where an arched entrance took them into the large, well-furnished kitchen. Through the generous windows Bolan could see expansive, well-laid-out gardens.

The kitchen was a mix of traditional and modern. It even had a beamed ceiling. Clair offered Bolan a seat at a large kitchen table while she filled mugs with coffee from a gently simmering percolator. She slid one mug in front of him, then sat facing him across the table.

She waited until Bolan had tasted the coffee.

"Verdict?"

"It's good," he said.

"So…Ethan," she said. "Are we going to swap information?"

"How much do you know about his current involvement?"

"In the OrgCrime force?" And when Bolan nodded she said, "Ethan only tells me what he can. He doesn't go into too much detail. The unit's work isn't a secret as such. There are articles in the media. Not detailed operational stuff, of course, but stories about how the combined force is trying to bring down these criminals."

"You have contact with Ethan?"

"I used to hear from him regularly. Mostly phone calls. Then he would turn up on the doorstep and stay for a day. Sometimes only for a few hours. But then all that stopped. Nothing. I had an emergency number I could call in London, but that didn't get me far. After a couple of times I got the feeling I was being fobbed off. I was told Ethan was on assignment and he would make contact when he could." Clair drummed her fingers against the tabletop. "Mr. Cooper, I'm not stupid. I knew something wasn't quite right." She stared at him. "You suddenly showing up is just confirming it, right?"

"I'm looking for Ethan because he's disappeared," Bolan said.

"*Disappeared?* How? Where?" Her voice was taut as she made a brave effort to hold it together. "My God, is he dead?"

"I don't think so."

"But you don't have *definite* proof?"

Bolan saw the way she was gripping the coffee mug, her knuckles white from the pressure. A hint of tears shone in her eyes.

"Be honest with me, Mr. Cooper. Tell me what you know."

"I won't lie. There's been an incident. Two members of the OrgCrime force have been killed. Shortly after that Ethan vanished."

"When you say *killed*… How?"

"Shot. Gangland-style. A bullet through the back of the head. The bodies left where they could easily be found. A warning to the OrgCrime force to back off."

Clair took a breath, ran a hand across her mouth. "How do you know the same hasn't happened to Ethan?"

"I don't for certain, but my instincts tell me not. If Ethan had been executed his body would most likely be exhibited just like the others. It hasn't. My guess is he was sharp enough to evade the hit team and go into hiding."

"Maybe he's hurt. Can't make contact. Isn't that possible? But we can't be sure, can we?"

Bolan noted the faint trace of panic in her voice. He didn't blame her for that.

"No, not for certain."

"Mr. Cooper…"

"Let's hold back until I can make some inquiries. First, you stop with the Mr. Cooper. The name is Matt. And I could go another mug of your coffee."

"Okay, Matt, coffee coming up." She poured it into his mug. "Can I ask just who you work for? If you're not with the OrgCrime unit, who are you with?"

Bolan smiled. "You can ask, Clair, but I don't have an answer you would understand. Let's just say I perform a necessary function for the good guys."

Her laugh was genuine. "Ambiguous at least." Then her gaze wandered, eyes growing wide.

Bolan realized his jacket had gaped enough to expose the holstered Beretta.

Clair fixed her eyes on his expressionless face. "Well, that explains a lot," she said.

"I don't go up against sweet old ladies."

"Well, I should have guessed, I suppose." She cleared her throat. "Seeing the gun makes me realize just how serious a mess Ethan could be in."

"I'll do whatever I can to find him."

The young woman nodded. "I know you will."

Bolan drank his coffee, falling silent as he went over something that had been skittering around on the fringes of his mind since he had entered the house.

"Clair, have there been any unusual incidents taking place recently?"

"Such as?"

"Strangers? Unknown vehicles on the road?"

"Nothing I can recall. Why? Should I be worried?"

"I just want to make sure."

The memory of the parked SUV came up.

Okay, Bolan told himself, *it could be nothing.*

A guy checking his maps for directions. Taking a break after a long drive. Maybe someone having a little personal time with his lady friend.

On the darker side of the coin the driver of the parked SUV might have been waiting for an opportunity to pay Clair a call.

Bolan had that anticipatory feeling he had experienced too many times. A growing sensation that things might be moving along on a new track. Since his strike at the airfield and his visit to Don Lawrence's apartment, the opposition might be upping their own game. Wanting to take stock of an unsettling situation.

"Clair, do you trust me enough to do what I'm going to ask next?"

"If Ethan trusted you there's no question."

"This is what we do then…"

8

Delbert watched as the tall, dark-haired guy left the house, Sorin's sister standing at the door and seeing him off. The guy fit the description Lawrence had given. There was no mistaking the size of the man, the confident way he carried himself. Delbert watched as the guy got into the car, offered a brief wave, then drove off. The girl stood watching until he vanished, then went back inside the house.

Taking out his cell Delbert called Corrigan.

"The son of a bitch was just at the sister's place. Big mother. Six foot plus. Looks like he could handle himself. Just like Lawrence described."

"He still there?"

"Uh-uh. Just got in his car and wheeled out."

"Our boy gets around," Corrigan said.

"Sorin still my priority?"

"Until I say different."

"I'll go make talk with the sister."

"Del, do what you need to. Just get her to spill *before* you put her out of her misery."

"I can do that."

Delbert completed the call and put away the cell. He opened the glove box and checked the suppressed Glock autopistol and the scalpel in its slim sheath. He had found that the minute people saw a cold, gleaming scalpel blade they became extremely cooperative very quickly; surgical steel might not have instant killing power, but when Delbert wanted answers he needed something to enforce his questions in a less brutal way. He slid the Glock into the custom shoulder rig under his jacket and the scalpel in the side pocket.

He studied the layout of house and stables from his vantage point, parked off the road on the wide grass verge, a stand of trees with drooping branches shading his vehicle. He used a pair of powerful binoculars to move between the buildings. There seemed to be only one employee at the stable. A slim young woman seeing to the stabled horses. Delbert saw her finish her tasks, then walk to the house and go inside. She emerged a few minutes later and moved out of sight down the side of the house. Shortly after, a bright red Mini Cooper drove into sight. It rolled down the drive, turned left and picked up speed as it went down the quiet road.

"Delbert, my brother, now is the time."

He fired up the SUV and swung onto the road, drove up to the gate and along the drive. He parked at the side of the house and climbed out. Apart from the occasional horse noises from the stable, the place was enveloped in a hushed silence.

Delbert walked to the front door. It stood open and he could see the hall, the wood floor polished and gleaming. As he stepped over the threshold he picked up the sound of a clock ticking. A sonorous tone that spoke of money and permanency.

His soft-soled shoes made no sound as he moved along the hall, checking out each door as he passed. A large, well-furnished living room that looked out on the drive. Empty. At the far end of the hall he could make out the kitchen. Then he reached another open door on his right. Before he got to the entrance he saw that the wall shelves were filled with books.

Library?
Office?

A large oak desk stood in the wide bay window that looked across at the stables. A computer sat on the desk. The woman he had seen talking to her recent visitor was seated at the desk, concentrating on the spread of papers in front of her. She still had on the same clothes she'd been wearing earlier—a sweater, tight jodhpurs and leather riding boots. Delbert smiled. He could always appreciate a good-looking woman.

Especially if he might have to interrogate her.

Delbert reached into his pocket and drew out the sheathed scalpel. He slid the blade free, dropping the sheath back into his pocket as he crossed the floor. He got to within a couple of feet of the seated woman.

That was when she spoke.

"Your reflection in the window has given you away," she said in an even tone.

Delbert dropped his free hand on her shoulder, fingers squeezing hard into her flesh. He was annoyed with himself for making such an error.

"Not going to save you though," he said. "I got questions about your brother you need to answer, bitch, and if I don't get what I need… Well, let's say I'll cut your pretty face into bloody ribbons."

"You'd hurt me?" Clair Sorin said.

"Damn right."

"Wrong," a quiet voice said from just behind Delbert.

Confusion held Delbert for a couple of seconds, but before he even turned he knew who he would see.

The big, dark-haired man who had driven away from the house. The guy Delbert had watched vanish along the quiet country road. Son of a bitch must have parked some distance away and walked back, coming in through the rear of the house.

Delbert pivoted on one foot, the scalpel extended as he caught a glimpse of the big American. Delbert slashed the blade at him, intending a swift cut across the throat. The move didn't even make it to the halfway point. Bolan's hands swept up in a defensive arc. The right caught Delbert's wrist just below the hand, twisting hard so that bones moved, wrenched out of place. Delbert gasped, letting go of the scalpel as his fingers became numb. He was more used to inflicting pain than receiving it. Bolan's left hand also moved. Bunched into a large fist it slammed into Delbert's nose, crushing it into a blood-spurting mess. Delbert expelled a wild roar of pain. He swung his left at the big guy, intending to land a telling blow, but Bolan swayed to one side, avoiding the fist. He lashed out with his right foot, slamming it against Delbert's right knee. The kick was delivered with all of Bolan's muscular weight behind it. Delbert's knee simply collapsed under the crippling impact, and everything beneath the flesh turned to mush. The blow had totally pulverized Delbert's knee. He let out an agonized scream as he went down, hugging his ruined limb, any malicious thoughts directed at Clair and Bolan forgotten in his new world of all-enveloping pain.

Bolan bent and frisked the man. He found Delbert's suppressed Glock and his cell. He dropped the pistol and the phone on Clair's desk, then retrieved the discarded scalpel and placed it next to the gun. When Clair saw it she was unable to repress a shudder.

"Would he really have used it?" she asked, because this sudden world of violence had no place in her life.

"These people have no respect for life," Bolan said. "This is how they operate. And, yes, he would have used it."

Clair's face was bloodless and she was suddenly trembling with shock.

"And what about you, Matt Cooper? You don't come across as an advocate of moderation."

"What should I have done, Clair? Reasoned with him? Tried to talk him down?"

Her cheeks flushed. "I meant… Oh, dammit, I don't know what I meant. You just saved me from God knows what and here I am preaching at you." She stepped close, impulsively throwing her arms around Bolan's neck and hugging him. "I'm sorry. It's just…" And then she began to sob, her body heaving as reaction to the situation took over.

Bolan held her gently to him. He understood. Her quiet, settled life had been invaded by a violent turn of events she had never witnessed before. She was entitled to be upset. The resentment would come later—the anger directed toward the people responsible for this incident. That would be when Bolan might gain some insight into Ethan Sorin's whereabouts. No guarantees, but Mack Bolan always hoped that something good might come from initial setbacks.

Delbert's pained sounds had reduced to a low moan. He hugged his shattered knee and bled from his broken nose.

Clair's intense grip on Bolan slackened as she brought herself under control. She remained close, her warmth and the scent of her perfume not unpleasant sensations. Her hair stroked his cheek, reminding Bolan how often he missed out on life's more simple pleasures.

She cleared her throat. "Matt, I'll be fine now."

"Don't rush on my account," he said gently.

She raised her head and stared at him. Despite the tears that moistened her cheeks she still managed to look beautiful.

"I...should thank you for what you just did." Clair kissed him on the cheek, her lips remaining for long seconds before she stepped slowly away from him.

"Thank you, Matt." A moan from Delbert caught her attention and she stared down at the man. "What happens to him now?"

"He'll be taken care of," Bolan said.

"I don't know if I care for whatever that means."

"I'm going to call the people Ethan works for. They'll handle him. Ask him the right questions. Just remember who he works for."

"Bad people?"

"The worst."

She nodded. "Okay."

"This guy showing up goes a long way to prove what I've been thinking. If Ethan were dead they'd have no reason to try to get to you, asking questions."

"You mean they don't know where Ethan is, either?"

"Seems likely."

"That's good, isn't it?"

Bolan nodded. "Hey, I think we both could do with some of that coffee we had before."

Clair looked at him. "A hint for me to leave you alone?"

Bolan held up the cell he'd retrieved from Delbert.

"I need to make a call."

Clair nodded and walked out of the room, closing the door behind her.

Bolan checked the phone, locating the call log. The last call Delbert had made was very recent. Bolan figured the time must have been shortly before he made his visit to the house. Bolan hit the redial key and listened as the phone rang. The call was answered after the fourth ring.

"Del? If you got her to talk already that's fast."

"Del fell down on the job," Bolan said. "His next stop will be a cell somewhere not very pleasant."

"Who is this?"

"Think about Don Lawrence. Your pickup crew at the airfield. Getting the picture now? And I'm only just getting warmed up."

"Do you really believe you can do us any real harm? We are bigger than one man."

"Just keep sending me idiots like Del and we'll see."

"Son of a bitch, we'll get to you. We'll get to Sorin, too. He can run but it doesn't matter where. We'll find him."

"I'll take that into consideration," Bolan said. "Just pass my message on to your board of directors. The numbers are already falling and they're due for retirement. The permanent kind of retirement."

Bolan cut the call and switched the cell off.

Delbert was staring up at him, his face gleaming with sweat from the pain in his knee.

"Something to contribute, Del?"

"They won't let go," the fallen man said. "They got people all over."

Bolan managed a smile. "If they expect to get anywhere, Del, let's hope they're better and smarter than you."

Taking out his own cell Bolan called Henning.

"I'm at Clair Sorin's place. She had an unwelcome visitor. The kind who uses a suppressed Glock and a scalpel as calling cards. Big guy who calls himself Delbert. He's likely to be on your most-wanted list. Now you've got him. He threatened Clair with the scalpel if she didn't tell him where her brother is."

"She okay?"

"Fine now. You want to send some of your people over to take him away? They might be able to gain some useful information if they get him to talk."

Henning drew breath. "Bloody hell, Cooper, you mean he's still alive? You getting soft in your old age?"

"I might be hurt at that remark if I didn't know you were being facetious. We had a little scuffle, but Delbert is alive. Better send your medic along, though. Del has a sore knee and nose, is all."

Henning chuckled. "Yeah, right."

"I haven't mentioned moving to Clair yet," Bolan said, "but I know she won't go, so a protection team might be in order."

"She'll get one," Henning said. "We look after our own. I'll make sure she gets the best."

"You just do that."

"You'll stay around until Clair is covered?"

Bolan told him yes and they finished the call.

IT TOOK THE TEAM just under an hour to show up. Two SUVs with four people in each and a third vehicle that turned out to have a couple of paramedics on board. As they emerged from the vehicles Bolan saw they were all well-armed with a combination of handguns and SMGs

"Henning told us to ask for Cooper," the team leader said when Bolan met them at the door. "That you? I'm Tom Hanley."

Bolan nodded. "In here," he said and led them into the kitchen where Delbert was seated on a wooden chair, secured with duct tape.

"I want my lawyer," Delbert demanded. "I got rights."

The team leader managed a tight grin. "Funny how they all get righteous when they get caught." He glanced at Delbert. "You got it wrong. We don't do lawyers. You, my son, are on your own."

Bolan said, "He threatened Miss Sorin with the Glock and the scalpel."

"Fuck you," Delbert said. "You can't prove a damn thing."

"Del, you wearing gloves?"

"What?"

"I can see you're not. So your prints are all over those items."

Delbert scowled. "He attacked me, man. Broke my nose and my fucking knee."

"Fellers," Hanley said to the medics, "deal with this piece of garbage. I want him ready to travel in ten minutes. He gives you any lip fill him full of tranquilizers."

"Where you taking me?" Delbert asked.

Hanley shook his head. "Somewhere you don't want to know about."

"I don't mind if you drop him on the way out," Clair said. She had stood aside during the initial appearance of the team, but now she reached out to shake Hanley's hand. "I'm glad to see you and your people."

"Good to see you're unharmed."

"Thanks to Matt. If he hadn't been here I hate to think how this might have turned out."

"Henning said you're looking for Ethan." Hanley checked the tall American. "This some new angle? I mean, you're not on any of the OrgCrime teams I know."

Bolan smiled. It was a question asked of him on any number of occasions. "Let's just say I work the game a different way."

"Henning said not to ask too many questions. He said you were on the right side though." Hanley glanced across at Delbert. "Can't argue about that."

Things moved quickly after that.

Delbert, still protesting and threatening, was taken out to the paramedics' vehicle and driven away.

Hanley's team established themselves in a room Clair led them to. There were already CCTV cameras attached to the house and stables, so the team simply tapped in using digital connections. They had a number of flat-screen monitors displaying images.

"Please don't tell me you have a helicopter overhead as well," Clair said drily.

Hanley grinned. "See what she's like, Cooper. How can you deal with her?" He added, "Actually, Miss Smarty Pants, we can connect to a satellite feed if we need to."

"I'm impressed," Clair said.

"There will also be a protection team around 24/7 until we resolve this problem. Inside the house and around the grounds."

Clair made a glum face. "Oh, God," she said. "That means I'll be making pots of tea day and night."

"Don't forget the bacon sandwiches," Hanley said.

Clair touched his arm. "Thank you. I mean it."

"No problem, love. That brother of yours would make my life hell if we didn't look after you."

Hanley took Bolan aside and they wandered outside.

"We'll make sure she stays safe," he said.

"I never doubted it," Bolan said.

"Schiller and Cobb being killed the way they were... Bloody hell, they were *executed*. It hit the OrgCrime squad hard. Then Ethan vanishing kind of topped it off. These bastards are just showing us they don't respect us. Don't recognize us as any threat. Trouble is, our hands are tied by so much damned legislation and red tape we have to get signed off before we even think about making moves. We make headway on paper, but that's as far as it gets. We have the information but it's like we're toothless." Hanley stopped and turned to face Bolan. "When we heard what had happened at the airfield there was a bloody great cheer in our office. Cooper, I can't claim to understand who or what you are. The hell with that. If you can keep hitting these bastards, you go on doing it. Any help I can offer, just call."

Bolan nodded. "I might take you up on that." He turned and pointed at the dark blue SUV. "That's Delbert's. You mind if I take a look inside?"

"I'll come with you. We might find something useful."

The SUV looked clean. There didn't appear to be anything left behind that might provide information.

"Tidy bugger, isn't he?" Hanley observed.

One of his team called and Hanley excused himself and crossed to speak to the man.

Bolan slid into the driver's seat and tapped the SatNav. He scanned the list, checking the one titled Home. It gave a Postal Code, the British version of the Zip Code. Bolan memorized the code. It was a start.

He made his way back inside the house and found Clair seated back at her desk, idly tapping at her computer keyboard. She glanced up at him.

"I have something that might be useful," she said. "But I only want *you* to know."

"About Ethan?"

"Yes."

"Here," she said, handing him a folded sheet of paper. "If Ethan is desperate he might go here."

"Family secret?"

Clair smiled. "You could say that. It was a refuge we used to go to years ago. We kept it to ourselves. Somewhere the family could go when we needed to get away. We never told anyone. Never invited guests." She touched Bolan's hand. "It might be a waste of time, but I couldn't think of anywhere else Ethan might go."

"We'll see." Bolan pocketed the note.

Clair stood up, eyes searching his face. "Will I see you again?"

"It could happen."

"I'd like to find out more about Matt Cooper."

"I'm not all that interesting."

She shook her head. "I don't think that's entirely true."

"Time I moved on. You going to be okay?"

"I think so." This time the smile was a little forced. "Not that I have much choice. At least I won't be lonely. Not with the protection team around." She hugged Bolan. "Thank you. Again."

He held her for a moment.

"Mmm, I really do think it's time you left," Clair said with little conviction.

9

The postal code from Delbert's phone led Bolan to an address in South Hampstead, a residential area of London. Solid houses stood on tree-lined streets. Bolan cruised the area until he found a place to park. Not an easy call in the densely populated district. He had checked it out on his way and the street was designated as non-regulated—the last thing he needed was to return and find his vehicle had been towed away, or fitted with a clamp.

He slipped into the shadows and worked his way back to the house. Under his long coat Bolan wore his blacksuit. He carried the Beretta and had a knife sheathed on his hip. The darkness, broken by pools of light from streetlamps, helped to minimize his presence. Bolan was thankful for the light drizzle—the rain discouraged most people from walking the streets.

Reaching the house, he took note of light behind windows and a couple of cars parked inside the perimeter wall. Bolan slipped past the vehicles and down the side of the house. He kept moving, reaching the rear. There was a garden, slightly overgrown, and an exterior light threw a pale spread of illumination out across the paved area. Bolan eased across to the first rear window. He checked the room—brightly lit and set out as a dining room. Three men sat around the table, playing cards. They were all armed. One wore a shoulder rig, the others had autopistols in hip holsters. Bottles of beer stood on the table and smoke from cigarettes had already created a shifting haze above their heads. Bolan could hear the low murmur of voices and the occasional burst of laughter.

He ducked below the sill and moved to the rear door. Another window showed him the kitchen, a single light revealing it was empty. Bolan slipped the 93-R from its holster and set it for single shot. He checked the rear door—it gave at his touch. He pushed it open far enough to allow him to slip inside. A short hallway with doors on each side. The one for the card-players' room was on his left. It was partly open and Bolan could hear loud voices. A heated conversation that stopped short of an argument.

"…feel like we're just sitting around for Corrigan's convenience. Him and his fuckin' team swan around like royalty. They use this house like it was a hotel. Order us around like we're just hired help."

"Well-paid hired help, so stop moaning, Eames."

"All I'm saying is we should be doing more."

"Bloody hell, Eames, maybe you'd be happier where Delbert is. He gets caught by the cops and now he's sitting in a cell God knows where."

"So much for being on Corrigan's team," a third voice said. "At least it shows they can screw up just like everyone else."

Eames said, "Ask me there's been too much screwing up the last few days. The pickup crew getting hit. Then Lawrence's minder getting himself dead. I mean, what's going on?"

"Tell you what, Eames, you can ask this mystery bloke yourself if he shows up."

Bolan moved on cue, edging the door open, and stepped into the room. As he flattened against the wall, his Beretta covering the card playing trio, he pushed the door shut with his free hand.

"Now's the time if you have questions," he said.

Individuals caught in such a moment of indecision go one of two ways—either they figure that in such a position it's better to take with the cautious approach and survive, or they say to hell with the safe option and go for the dangerous route.

Bolan's combat senses warned him at least one of the men at the table was taking the riskier route microseconds before it happened.

He saw the guy wearing the shoulder rig tense up, his facial expression a mix of bravado and *what-the-hell-am-I-doing* as he snatched at the autopistol. The thug even managed to half draw the piece, starting to twist in his seat, before Bolan turned the Beretta and triggered a single 9 mm Parabellum round. The slug struck just above the target's left ear. It cored through bone and brain, deforming on its route so that when it blew out on the opposite side of the skull it took a sizable portion of the head with it.

Movement on Bolan's immediate left warned him of another threat. He saw the seated figure raising the handgun from its hip holster. He dropped to a crouch, tracking the 93-R and triggered a pair of shots into the man's chest. The impact pushed him against the back of the chair, tipping it off balance. As the guy went backward his finger jerked the trigger of his part-drawn weapon and the slug burned into his own hip.

Still in a low crouch Bolan caught the third man leveling his weapon across the tabletop, panic in his eyes as he desperately made his shot. The slug plowed into the plaster wall a foot above Bolan's head, then the big American returned fire. Three fast shots. His 9 mm slugs, angled upward, tore through the tabletop, showering splinters of wood in the air. They hit the shooter in the throat, tearing large, ragged holes as they tunneled up through his flesh and lodged in his brain. Jets of bright blood burst from the target's ravaged throat, spurting across the tabletop.

Bolan straightened up. He shook his head—this wasn't how he had wanted it to go. Dead men couldn't talk. Information would have been more useful than three corpses. But they had chosen their way.

Turning to the door, Bolan cracked it open and stood listening. There were no sounds from the rest of the house. He waited before he emerged and made his way to the front. A quick check of the rooms confirmed there were no more occupants on the ground floor. Bolan crossed to the stairs. He went up fast, pausing on the landing.

Now he *did* hear sounds. Muffled and coming from bedrooms to his right.

Bolan checked the first door. He turned the knob and pushed the door open, standing to the side in case of a threat.

He had no need.

The room's single occupant posed no danger.

A young woman, her left wrist handcuffed to the metal bed headboard, stared at him with large, wide-open eyes.

"Help me," she said. *"Please help me."*

"MY NAME IS LEINA RAJIC," the girl had said.

Bolan then left her only long enough to go back downstairs and search the bodies, looking for keys—he found a number of them on a metal ring. He returned upstairs and began going through the different keys. On the third attempt the cuff opened. The flesh where the cuff had gripped was raw and broken.

"How long have you been here?" Bolan asked.

"Around three weeks. Before that I was in another house with other girls. They kept us chained there, too." She plucked at the plain, sleeveless dress she was wearing. "They made us wear these things. Took away our clothes and shoes."

"Where did they bring you from?"

"I came from Albania. There were eight of us when we were taken. Only seven reached here. One girl died because she kept trying to escape. She would not stop. One of the men beat her to death in front of us as an example. We were on some ship. They made us watch while they wrapped her body in chains and threw her overboard."

"Are there any others here with you?"

Leina nodded. "In the next two rooms. Next door, the girl, Tira, is only seventeen."

"Come with me," Bolan said. "Why were the three of you brought here?"

"For the amusement of the men who work in this place." Leina managed a thin smile. "They use us whenever they want."

"Not anymore," Bolan said. He handed Leina the keys. "Free the others. I need to check the house."

"Are you from police?"

"Not officially. But you'll be looked after now. I promise."

Leina's eyes studied him. The expression in them suggested she doubted what he said. Bolan could understand her skepticism. After what she had been through, her trust, especially in men, must have reached an all-time low.

"The three men who held you here are dead. You can take a look if you need to. I'm trying to put an end to what their mob does."

"You tell the truth?"

"Yes. One of my failings is I never lie. I'm going to call the authorities and let them know where you are. They'll take you to a safe place. Leina, tell them everything you know. Their job is to try and put these people down, so they need all the information they can get. A man named Henning will help you through this."

She nodded in understanding. "All right. Are you not staying?"

"No. I have to find someone. A friend. I can't become involved with the authorities."

"What do I tell police about you?"

Bolan shrugged. "Whatever you have to. Now go and free your friends while I make my call."

10

Bolan was halfway across the landing when he heard the rattle of the front door. A voice called out. When there was no reply the owner of the voice strode across the hall, passing out of Bolan's sight as he went toward the rear of the house. Bolan heard a muffled outburst as the three dead men were discovered. The man ran back toward the front door. Bolan caught a glimpse of a weapon in his hand as he jerked the door wide and called out.

"Get in here fast. Looks like we've been hit."

Bolan flattened against the landing wall. This time the numbers were falling the wrong way, leaving him trapped with three innocent young women to protect.

He didn't dwell on the problem. It needed a solution and the Executioner was never one to shrink from any kind of awkward predicament. He had his Beretta and an extra clip in his pocket.

Peering around the corner of the wall he saw the guy who had first entered, presently reinforced by two more armed men. The last man in shouldered the front door shut.

"Upstairs, Phil. Check the bitches. Monty, with me. Go."

The one named Phil started up the stairs, his handgun held across his chest, left hand pulling on the banister rail.

Bolan let him reach the head of the stairs before he stepped out and delivered a brutal backfist to the man's throat. It was full-on, with no holding back, and Phil uttered a single, gargled cry before his crushed throat shut down. He toppled backward, frantically trying to maintained his balance. He failed. His windmilling arms and legs flailed in an attempt to keep him upright. He alternated between wall and banister, losing his gun and eventually losing his balance. He crashed down on his back, bouncing from stair to stair and coming to a halt at the bottom. His arms and legs lay in unnatural positions, as did his head and neck.

"What is noise?"

Leina came up behind Bolan. Behind her were the other two girls. They crowded against Leina, eyes questioning, alternately staring at Bolan's tall figure and Leina.

"Keep them back," Bolan said.

He eased back from the edge of the wall, a move that proved to be lifesaving as autopistols exploded from below and slugs tore chunks of plaster from the landing wall. Shreds of wallpaper and dust filled the air.

"You have called police?" Leina asked.

"No. I think the neighbors will do it for us if they hear those shots."

Bolan took out his phone and hit the speed dial for Henning. When the man came on the line Bolan didn't waste time on chitchat. He gave Henning the address and told him to send help.

"It's where Delbert was staying. I tangled with some of the outfit's local chapter. Found three young women brought here for their recreational needs. Chained to their beds. One speaks English—her name is Leina Rajic. I got them free. Just go easy on them. I just had three more armed hostiles turn up. Greg, I need to get out before your buddies arrive, so there might be more casualties."

"Do what you have to, and good luck."

Bolan put the cell away.

"Stay back," he warned Leina.

He had picked up a creak from the stairs. He heard the soft rustle of clothing and a low, hoarse whisper.

Bolan took a deep breath, gauged the distance he was going to have to travel, then launched himself in a powerful shoulder roll that took him across the gap at the top of the stairs and beyond.

A man yelled in surprise.

Bolan came to rest on one knee, the 93-R coming online as the two armed men swiveled in his direction. His move had left them lagging behind. Bolan aimed between the stair railings and lined up the lead guy. The Beretta spat its suppressed load, two 9 mm slugs catching him full-face. The man squealed, throwing his hands over his suddenly bloody face. He rose to his full height and turned half around before plunging back down to the hall. The surviving shooter, forced to pull away, spun back in Bolan's direction to find the big American at the head of the stairs, Beretta swinging on target.

"Put it away," Bolan said as the man moved his own weapon. "Last chance."

"I can take you, Yank."

The autopistol angled up.

The Beretta expended three fast shots. They hit the man in the chest, placed directly over the heart. One went all the way through and burst out the target's back. He fell without a sound, slithering down the stairs to curl into a ball at the bottom.

"They always believe they're indestructible," Bolan murmured softly.

"What do you say?"

It was Leina. She clutched at Bolan's arm, fingers tight against his coat.

"Nothing," Bolan said.

"You must go before police come," Leina said. "Go now. Quickly."

"Look after yourself and your friends, Leina Rajic."

She touched his face.

"Fat i mire," she whispered. "Good luck."

Bolan went down the stairs and through the house, leaving the way he had entered, by the rear door. He slipped the Beretta back into its holster, easing past the side of the house, then through the garden. He negotiated the fence, then tracked along the rear of the neighboring houses until he was able to reach the intersecting street. Keeping to the shadows between the wide-spaced streetlights he came to the main road again and located his parked car.

As he unlocked the door he picked up the distant sound of police sirens. They were quickly becoming louder. Looking in the rearview mirror he could make out figures starting to congregate around the house he had just vacated. Beyond the gathering crowd he saw the blue flash of police cruisers at the far end of the street. He started the car and eased into gear, freeing the parking brake. He kept the lights off as he eased away from the curb, crossing to the far side of the street. Once he was far enough not to be noticed, he switched on his lights and touched the gas pedal, picking up a little speed. At the far end of the street Bolan made a left, taking himself onto the main road leading away from Hampstead. He carefully merged with the traffic. More police cars, accompanied by ambulances, swept by, turning into the street Bolan had just quit.

"You'll be safe now, Leina," he murmured.

11

Henning shook his head as he surveyed the bloody scene. Three bodies at the back of the house. Three more at the foot of the stairs—two dead from bullet wounds, one from a broken neck, plus massive bruising to the throat. Cooper's clear-up rate was mounting rapidly, he thought.

"You're working overtime on this one, pal," Henning said to himself.

"You say something?" one of his men asked.

"No," Henning said. "Nothing important."

He was summoned upstairs and shown into one of the bedrooms.

A young woman sat on the bed, her left wrist handcuffed to the bed's headboard.

"Henning, two more in the other rooms," someone said.

"Get them free," Henning ordered.

He studied the girl. She held his gaze for a moment and Henning could have sworn he detected a ghost of a smile on her lips.

"You understand English?"

The girl nodded. "Yes. My name is Leina. Are we safe now? There was so much shooting. Men falling down stairs."

Henning was about to ask her how she knew that, but he understood. She had returned herself and the others to their manacled condition to distance them from having to say much about what had happened.

Damned if they aren't covering for Cooper, he thought. How does he manage to do that?

"Don't mention that falling down the stairs thing to anyone. Understand, Leina?"

"Yes, I understand."

"We'll get you out of here soon—have you checked over."

There was a moment's silence.

"Your friend. Will he be all right, Mr. Henning?"

Henning had to smile. "I believe he will."

Later, back downstairs, Henning stood in the hall. The bodies had been processed, and as much evidence as possible had been collected and taken away.

"Bloody mess, boss."

Henning nodded at the young OrgCrime agent. "At least the right bastards got themselves killed."

"Bit harsh."

"These buggers are so low on the scale, Marsh, they don't even register. You read all the data we have on them?"

"Yeah."

"So don't go wasting sympathy on them. You saw the condition of those women and girls out at the airfield. Two dead. Most of the others still needing medical attention. Three more here, chained to the beds. Are we still shedding tears, Marsh?"

"I guess not, boss."

"Remember that every day we're on this detail."

"We located a couple of laptops," one of the agents called.

"Get them to base. Go through them and pull every scrap of data you can. Maybe we'll come up with some hard evidence we can throw at these bastards."

HENNING WAS STILL at his desk as the light filtered through the blinds. Beyond the glass the city was waking to a new day. Henning couldn't have cared less. It had been a long night and his workload hadn't lessened by a fraction.

"Hey, boss, fresh coffee," a voice called out.

It was Marsh, carrying a tray holding mugs of steaming

liquid. He placed one in front of Henning, then moved on to distribute the rest of the coffee around the office.

"How can you be so bloody cheerful at this time of day?"

"Clean living," Marsh said.

Henning felt his burn phone vibrate in his pocket. When he answered he recognized the voice at the other end immediately.

"Thanks for the mess we had to clean up last night," he grumbled.

"Are the girls okay?" Bolan asked.

"They're fine. Being cared for in a safe environment."

"They'd better be," Bolan said, "or I'll come back to haunt you."

"Most of those beings no longer with us are in our database—they were all involved with the mob."

"Have you got any useful information from the scene?"

"We found a couple of laptop computers. They're with our cyber team as we speak."

"You find anything that might assist, I'd be grateful."

"Well, of course, Mr. Cooper, I'll have it sent directly to you via the UPS courier service."

"Do I sense a little testiness there?"

"It's been a crap night," Henning said. "A long, crap night."

"Sorry," Bolan apologized. "Didn't mean to come over strong. I know you're stepping across the line every time you help. But I need to find Ethan Sorin before the mob does. I won't let him die on my watch."

"Amen to that," Henning said. "I'll feed you anything I can. Now you just watch your back, Cooper."

"Always."

BOLAN ENDED THE CALL. He was back on the road after a night's rest at his hotel. He had been able to have a long, hot shower before falling into bed. Since leaving London he had been driving for hours, heading north, his destination the location Clair Sorin had given him.

He was hoping her information would get him to Ethan Sorin and that the man was still alive. Even though Clair had told him the location was a family secret, Bolan understood the frailty of maintaining total security, even with such an innocuous thing as a secret holiday destination. He understood the power the mob wielded, their ability to ferret out the smallest detail. Total security was something people wanted to exist, but in Bolan's experience it was hard to achieve. In reality, even governments had found that out to their cost.

12

Corrigan had an inquiring mind. It was constantly badgering him to explore the possibilities that existed in every situation. Just like the Sorin problem. The OrgCrime agent, along with his now dead partners, had infiltrated one of the mob's databases and had extracted information. Information that would have the potential to blow the organization wide open if it got into OrgCrime's hands. Against the odds they had walked away, albeit only for a short time, before they were located and dealt with. Two had died. The one called Sorin had eluded his pursuers and was presently in hiding. The information this agent held did not appear to have been passed to his group. But that was because it had become clear to Sorin that the OrgCrime unit had a mole in their ranks, and he was unsure whom to trust. However, currently there was an added complication—the unknown American who had made it clear he was intent on bringing the mob down. His initial hits had confirmed his intention. His discouraging success had stirred the top men into action and the problem had been assigned to Corrigan and his own team.

A brief, but accurate summation as far as Corrigan was concerned. Unfortunately matters had taken an unexpected and disturbing twist.

Delbert, previously a reliable and experienced operative, had let himself be taken by the American when he had confronted Sorin's sister. Corrigan had received an update from his OrgCrime informer. Delbert had been arrested and whisked off to a covert location where he would be questioned and kept in a secure lockdown. The man was a write-off. Out of the picture. Corrigan accepted the situation because he had no choice and also because if Delbert had let himself be taken then he was on his own. Corrigan had no patience with failure.

He recalled the brief cell phone call from the American. The man had been calm, precise in his telling of what had happened to Delbert. Corrigan had to admire his nerve. The way he had suggested Corrigan relay his words to the mob's top men. The guy was no rampant vigilante—he was deadly serious. A smile crossed Corrigan's face as he replayed the reactions of the bosses during the video conference. There was outrage and a little panic. Then the recriminations from some of them, accusing Corrigan of not doing his job, until he quietly reminded them he had only just taken on the assignment, and if they wanted to handle it themselves he would step aside. It took Tony Lowell to bring the stress level down. Lowell had the touch of the old school about him. He might have been the elder statesman within the mob but that only lent him authority, and he had applied his experience to the situation.

"Give the guy a chance," he had said. *"Corrigan has never failed us before. He's the best. But he's digging in the dark here. Before he can get rid of this guy he needs to identify him. And right now not one of us has any idea who this bastard is. You don't snap your fingers and expect the guy to pop up out of nowhere. Let Corrigan do his job. Give him some stretch. You people need to think before you start throwing dirt...."*

Now, Corrigan sat in his apartment, behind his desk. He had been busy for the last few hours, concentrating on matters at hand.

He had been tasked with the need to eliminate the mystery man interfering with operations.

And with the capture of Ethan Sorin.

As much as he wanted to get his hands on the elusive Yank, Corrigan's main concern was Sorin, who had escaped being taken out like his partners and had gone into hiding, along with the data the three OrgCrime agents had gathered. If the OrgCrime unit got their hands on that information they would have the means to strike down the mob.

Delbert's attempt to reach Sorin's sister had ended in failure. So Corrigan had to deal with the matter again.

He saw two ways to approach it.

Locate and go directly for Sorin.

Or take the sister away from the OrgCrime protection team. With Clair Sorin in the hands of the mob they would have a bargaining chip. Something to force Sorin to come forward and hand over the stolen data.

Corrigan didn't fool himself into imagining either way would be easy. There were no guarantees of success one way or the other. But something needed to be done.

He decided to try the direct approach first. Try and find where the agent had gone.

That was when Corrigan came up with a potentially workable theory. He would have been the first to admit it was way off the line, but right then he needed anything to offer him a chance of locating Sorin. So he threw the dice and waited to see if he hit the right combination.

Corrigan made use of his *own* assets. He had built up a background file of people skilled in a number of applications. Phone tappers. Cyber hackers. Watchers and listeners. They were paid well for their services—money was no problem. The mob understood the importance of good intelligence and allowed Corrigan to operate in that field.

At this moment Corrigan had his people working full-time on the Sorin problem. He was attacking it from all angles and felt he had everything covered.

His laptop pinged as a message entered his email inbox. Corrigan opened it.

The email told him to check the attachment. When he did, Corrigan was presented with telephone bills going back a number of years and a similar number of bank statements.

When he scrolled through the lists he saw that there were highlighted entries.

He picked up his throwaway cell and called a number. His call was answered after two rings.

"I got your email, Rankin," Corrigan said. "You want to decipher it for me?"

Rankin said, "I ran all the permutations of Sorin's background. Pulled up details of his home phone number and hacked into his bank account. Banks are so easy to get into. I downloaded bills and statements then got out of those places before anyone even knew I'd been there. I compared dates and times and came up with a few constants. I checked phone numbers and lucked onto one that wasn't used much, but when I ran the address for that number it turned out to be located outside a small village in the northeast of Scotland. Google Earth maps has a picture. Isolated house on the edge of a loch."

"Who owns the place?"

"Land Registry holds titles to properties. The house has been in the Sorin family for over thirty years. Current owner is Ethan Sorin. Once I had that it was easy to locate utility payments via Sorin's bank statements."

"Rankin, you are almost worth the money I pay you."

"Oh, I know that."

"I'll transfer your fee shortly. And thanks."

Corrigan put down the phone, leaning back in his leather executive chair, smiling to himself.

His pleasure was short-lived after he picked up the ringing telephone on his desk.

"*Yeah?* Talk to me."

The call was short and to the point.

The house in Hampstead had been hit. Six crew-member fatalities. The three women being held there were currently in police hands and the house was under investigation by the OrgCrime unit. The informant had learned that when the house was searched a couple of laptop computers had been seized and taken back to the OrgCrime unit for investigation.

"Sonofabitch," Corrigan yelled across the apartment.

His immediate thoughts were directed at the big American. The guy was showing up everywhere.

But who the hell was he?

Corrigan pushed to his feet and crossed to the liquor cabinet. He poured himself a large whisky—very large. He took a long swallow and noticed his hand was shaking slightly. It wasn't from fear. It was plain and simple frustration. Corrigan liked to be in control. At this moment he wasn't. The mysterious American had the upper hand for the time being. Corrigan emptied the tumbler, placed it back on the cabinet and returned to his desk.

He conceded that the American appeared to be doing exactly what he had threatened—attacking the mob and taking it apart piece by piece. His skill was in gaining information and using it well. He made no announcements. No prior warnings. He seemingly came out of nowhere, carried out his strike and then simply vanished. The guy was like a ninja. Whatever he was, the guy was good. And he had no qualms when it came to handing out his kill shots.

Locate your enemy.

Make your hit.

Leave no prisoners.

Except in Delbert's case.

Corrigan figured the American must have decided that leaving Delbert alive might offer the OrgCrime unit someone to question in order to get information. Another point in his profile. The guy was ruthless but he was also smart. Thinking ahead. As he had when he'd left some of the crew at the airfield alive. Leaving them alive meant they were possible avenues for information once they were in the hands of the OrgCrime agency.

Corrigan made a call.

"I want a chopper ready ASAP. Three guys. Armed. I have a lead on Benson. We need to act on it fast because I have a feeling that fucking Yank might be on his way there, too.

Yes, *that* Yank. I'm working on the thought that Benson's sister might have pointed him in the right direction. His time might be up if we figure it correctly. No dodging the bullet for him this time."

Corrigan utilized his authority to organize a backup plan. He knew that the best operations could go belly-up, and if that happened they were back at the starting gate. So it was wise to have an alternative strategy. And that meant arranging to work on his other option.

Clair Sorin.

The sister.

But this time it would not be a one-man operation.

Corrigan made two more calls.

The first was to his OrgCrime inside man. It was a simple request. He wanted to know the strength of the protection team at Clair Sorin's house.

His follow-up call was to Nate Reese, one of his soldiers. Corrigan told him the background and the force he would be up against.

"Get yourself an armed team together. Get into position and wait for my call. If our boys make good and grab Sorin, I'll stand you down. If the hit doesn't come through you go in and take out the OrgCrime protection team. I want Sorin's sister alive. She can be our insurance. One way or another Sorin is going to give us what we want. If I have to skin that bitch in front of him I'll do it."

"Deadly force against the protection team?"

"Hell, yes. They won't want to lose Sorin's sister, so go in hard. Show those bastards the cost of standing up to us."

"You got it, boss," Reese said. "I'll let you know when we're set."

13

Northeast Scotland. Approaching the area Bolan was not surprised at the drop in temperature. The time of year and the location left a lot to be desired where the weather was concerned. This part of Scotland demanded fairly hardy inhabitants, the wind blowing in off the North Sea bringing squalls of chill rain. Bolan found himself driving through open, rugged terrain, with few signs of habitation the farther north and east he got. If this was where Ethan Sorin was in hiding he could not have chosen a more isolated spot.

The screen of the SatNav showed Bolan he was on track. The single strip of the road wound through the undulating landscape. Every now and then he spotted the dull gray of the sea off to his right. For the past hour he had seen only a few farms open to the elements. According to one of the few roadside signs he was about ten miles out from the village where Sorin's house was situated, though it was another eight miles to the east of the village itself. Bolan eased his tall frame in the seat. Comfortable as it was, he had been at the wheel for long hours. Despite the chill of the outside temperature, he had the climate control on, blowing cool air around the car. He had resisted opting for warmth in case it lulled him into lethargy. He did have the radio on, set low, and was listening to a music station that was beamed in from some Scandinavian source. The only Scottish stations he had been able to find were mostly filled with talk shows.

If Sorin was not at the house, Bolan would have to reconsider his approach. He had it fixed in his mind that there was no way he would quit. Sorin was in trouble and Bolan's determination to track him down would not diminish even if this particular route came to a dead end.

It was midafternoon when Bolan coasted through the village. A narrow street of well-preserved stone houses, a few small shops and a couple of pubs. There were lights showing from some windows against the cloudy day. A shivering spray of rain followed Bolan along the street and he was through the village almost before he realized. A few more houses hugged the road on the far side of the village, then even they vanished behind Bolan.

He heard the SatNav telling him he only had four miles to his destination. Bolan scanned the road ahead and found a place where he could park. He had on his blacksuit beneath his civilian clothing, which he shed. From the holdall in the passenger well, he retrieved his weapons.

The Beretta was snug in its holster, the sheathed combat blade against his hip. Bolan was hoping for a soft approach with a similar follow-up. His long experience called for caution and a prepared mind, because Mack Bolan understood the vagaries of fate. His visit here was to locate Sorin and ensure the man's safety. The protective voice at the back of his mind was warning him to go in on full alert, however, ready for any untoward situation. It was the way Bolan entered any unknown scenario. And his readiness was the main reason he had survived for so long. That and his well-honed responses to any threats. Bolan didn't spend too much time analyzing the complexities of his survival rate. He was who he was and that satisfied him.

Over the years he had been called many things. Some good, others not so much. But he never aspired to emulate any of the nicknames. He was, he supposed, an amalgam of them all. His nature led him to be what he was and to do what he did. He was not seeking accreditation for his actions. He had

declared his intentions way back and had maintained that resolve over his many campaigns. Nothing was going to alter
those conditions.

He rolled the car back onto the road and continued in the
direction his SatNav took him. He made the turn onto the
narrow, tarmac strip winding between tangled hedges. After
a quarter mile it opened out onto a graveled area fronting
the house. The stone-and-timber construction was old but
well kept. There was a ground and an upper floor, plus a
couple of outhouses to the right of the main structure. The
land sloped away at the rear of the house to the loch, where
the rain and the escalating wind disturbed the surface of the
water. On a bright sunlit day it would have presented an idyl-
lic view. On this day it was gray and uninspiring.

Bolan stopped the car and surveyed the house. There was
a dark gray SUV parked near the outhouses. Someone was
in the area. Bolan shut off the engine. Now he could hear
the rain on the metal roof and feel the slight tug of the wind.
There were no lights on. Windows in shadow. No movement.

For all he knew Sorin could be watching, wondering who
his visitor was.

Friend or foe?

In Sorin's position, Bolan would have wondered the same.
He leaned across and picked the long coat off the rear seat,
shrugging into it as he stepped from the car.

Bolan felt the wind against him, and the chill of the rain
against his face as he strode up to the house. At the front door
he rapped his knuckles against the weathered timber.

No response.

Bolan eased the 93-R from its holster, checking the setting
for single-shot action. He reached for the handle and pressed
it down. The door eased open on oiled hinges. Bolan pushed
it wide, stepping to the side, one shoulder against the solid
stone wall. From what he could see, the interior was shadowed. Silent.

"Ethan? Ethan Sorin? Show yourself. It's Cooper. Remember me? We made a good team, Ethan. Clair told me where I might find you. She's safe. Being looked after by your people."

The reaction was instant. A figure moved slowly into view, holding onto the door frame as he stepped into the light.

It was Sorin.

And he looked like he had just walked out of Hell.

14

The Bell helicopter belonged to the mob. Bought with the constant flow of money made by the various criminal activities, it was one of a number of aircraft, including a couple of Lear jets, the mob had on its books. There was another helicopter based in Europe and one more in the U.S.A. All on 24/7 standby, ready and waiting with flight crews. The U.K.-based Bell had picked up Corrigan's three-man team from a flight pad in London. Corrigan had called the pilot and read him the coordinates and the chopper lifted off immediately, heading north for Scotland.

Corrigan had sent along Markus, Pikey and Lapdog. Pikey and Lapdog were always ready for a fight. They had grown up on the streets, using natural cunning and their desire to survive to bring them through their early years as small-time crime had graduated to more extreme enterprises. They ran girls. Pushed drugs. Ventured into trafficking. They also had a penchant for terrifying violence, which they used without thought to what might result. All they understood was the effect the threat of violence had on their victims. It got them what they wanted. And it was as a form of punishment that they realized its potential. They both had a growing list of murders listed on their tallies. Truth be known they enjoyed their work, unfortunately to a level that even their contemporaries stepped away from. All except Corrigan. Once he had learned about them he delved into their past and saw what they might offer. He recruited them into the mob, honed their skills and his effect on them was strong. They enjoyed the power their new positions gave them, the security and the fact they belonged.

They sat back in the comfortable flight seats and looked forward to what lay ahead. Corrigan had run them through a refresher course on Sorin before they left. They knew as much about the man as anyone. Corrigan had laid out their mission brief in his apartment.

"If he's at the house, I want him alive. He has information that could hurt the organization. We don't know how much he carries inside his head, so Sorin dead is no good to us. His brains leaking all over the fucking heather is bad. Take him alive."

Lapdog's bony face showed a frown. "Can't we hurt him just a little, boss?" He was toying with the SMG in his skinny hands. "Seems a pity bringing these shooters if we can't use 'em."

"Have I ever said you are a scary psycho?" Corrigan said.

Lapdog grinned. "Thanks, boss."

"Pikey, keep him on a leash," Corrigan said.

"Sure thing."

Lapdog grunted in annoyance. He was still smarting from the fact that Corrigan had put Markus in command of the team. Markus had some military background and also had a steadier head on his shoulders.

Presently they were closing in on the target.

"Touchdown in five," the pilot said.

"Once you eyeball the house, land a couple of hundred yards away. Sorin may be armed," Markus said. "If he figures out who we are he might start capping a few rounds. I don't want the cost of repairing bullet holes coming out of my bonus."

"You think he might shoot at us?" Pikey asked with a sarcastic edge to his voice.

"For certain he isn't going to invite us in for tea and fuck-ing scones," Markus said.

Lapdog mumbled something under his breath. Like most bullies who enjoyed inflicting pain on others, he was not so brave when the possibility of harm to himself reared its head.

"Don't worry, Dog," Markus said. "If he does shoot you, I'll make sure you don't suffer too long."

Pikey laughed out loud. "See," he said, "Markus does care about you."

Lapdog slid down in his seat, hugging his SMG close to his skinny chest, eyes suddenly cold and hostile.

"There," the pilot said, pointing out through the rain-spattered canopy. "Target in sight."

Markus followed the man's pointing finger. Below he could see the outline of the house and outbuildings. He picked out the two cars parked next to the house.

"You got binoculars?" Markus asked the pilot.

"Under your seat."

Markus searched and found the glasses. "Bring her in from the front of the house. Slow and low. Pad and pen, Pikey. Write down what I tell you."

The pilot executed the maneuver and Markus leaned forward, scanning the parked cars. He quoted license numbers to Pikey who scribbled the pair of numbers down.

"Now what?" Lapdog asked.

Markus took out his sat phone and called Corrigan.

"I have two license plates I need identified." He read off the numbers. "How long?"

Corrigan chuckled, a derisory sound. "I'll put Rankin on it and make him sweat." He put Markus on hold and called Rankin. "Time to impress me." Corrigan quoted the license numbers. "Tell me who they belong to."

"One day, Corrigan, you are going to ask me the impos-sible. Not today, though," Rankin said. "The first plate be-longs to a rental vehicle. Belongs to a London franchise. The second is registered to an Ethan Sorin. Does that impress?"

"It does," Corrigan said. "I will arrange a bonus. Thanks."

Corrigan reconnected to Markus.

Markus said, "He get what you want, boss?"

"One of those cars is Sorin's. The other is a rental. From London."

"Our Yank?"

Corrigan smiled. "Maybe we can catch two for one."

The connection was ended.

"Put us down over there," Markus said, pointing out the wide, open space away from the house.

The chopper descended under the pilot's sure hand, despite the buffeting wind. It made a perfect landing. The pilot cut the power and the rotors began to slow.

"If you don't mind, I'll stay put," he said.

Markus gave a mirthless smile. "You do that." He opened his door. "Remember," he said to Pikey and Lapdog, "we need Sorin alive."

"Hey," Pikey said. "What if we find that fuckin' Yank *has* shown up?"

Markus's smile widened as he glanced across at Lapdog. "You can kill that son of a bitch as many times as you want. Now let's move."

Before they deplaned they each slipped on the lightweight digital comsets they had brought along. They ran quick checks to make sure they were all working and set to the same channel.

"Once we separate, keep in touch," Markus said.

The three men crossed the rain-streaked field, the soft ground pulling at their boots and coating them with mud. The waterproof coats resisted the rain and the hoods shielded their faces. The wind soughed in off the sea and they could taste salt in its moisture.

"If this is Scotland," Pikey said, "it sucks." He stepped in a shallow puddle. *"Shit."*

They drew into a huddle, the house no more than fifty

yards ahead. They were side-on to the building, so they could view front and rear.

"Lapdog, take the rear," Markus said. "Watch yourself. Sorin is a field agent. Not an old woman with a walking stick."

Lapdog nodded and veered off toward the house.

"He going to be all right?" Markus asked.

"Yeah. He's a pain but he knows his job," Pikey said.

"I can bloody hear you," Lapdog said over the comsets.

"Just watch your skinny arse, mate," Pikey said.

Markus made a final check of his SMG.

"Let's go," he said, and led the way across the final stretch of ground to the side of the house. They pressed against the wet stone, then edged their way to the front, moving past the parked cars.

"Front door," Markus said. "Stay below the window level. We hit the door and go straight in. Hard and fast before they know what's happening. Lapdog, you set?"

"Right by the kitchen door, boss."

"Be ready if Sorin tries to leave."

"He won't get by me."

Markus dropped to a crouch and led the way past the window, only straightening when he was positioned at the front door. He nodded to Pikey, who was on the other side of the door, SMG ready.

"Remember, we need Sorin alive. If you need to shoot, take an arm or a leg."

Markus moved so he was facing the door. He braced himself for the impact, then raised his right foot. He slammed the sole of his boot against the door, right in line with the handle. The door shivered, wood splitting. Markus struck it a second time and the door shattered and swung inward to crash against the wall.

"Go," Markus yelled. *"Go, go, go..."*

15

The man staring at Bolan bore little resemblance to the Ethan Sorin he had once known. Then, Sorin had been tanned and fit. Now, he was gaunt and had dark rings under his eyes. The blond hair was tangled and Sorin was unshaven and looked as if he had been sleeping in his clothes.

"Where did you come from? Bloody hell, you look like a fugitive from *The Matrix* in that coat."

"You mind if I get out of the rain?"

Sorin stepped aside as Bolan moved through the door. He closed it and turned to face his visitor.

"You said Clair was safe. Has she been in trouble? Because of me?" Sorin's voice rose in anger. "Have those bastards been trying to get to her?"

Bolan said, "Let's take it easy, Ethan. We need to talk things over." Bolan rook off the long coat and exposed his blacksuit and the holstered Beretta.

"I don't want to be unsociable, but most people bring a bottle of wine when they come calling, not a piece of artillery."

"I've already met your buddies from the mob, Ethan, and the last thing they want is to share a drink."

"You've got a point."

Sorin indicated for Bolan to cross the room to a fire burning in the stone hearth. The low-ceilinged room was neatly laid out with solid furniture.

"I just made coffee. You want some?"

Bolan nodded. He watched Sorin move to the hearth where a metal jug rested on the stone base. The Brit reached for one of the thick mugs hanging from hooks on the mantel. He filled the mug and handed it to Bolan. The big American didn't miss the slow, labored movements and the way Sorin favored his left side, reaching around to hug his ribs.

"Ethan, you need to see a doctor."

"I can't risk bringing anyone in. I'm reasonably safe here as long as no one can find me."

"*I* found you."

Sorin took his own mug and settled into a deep armchair.

"But you haven't come to put a bullet through the back of my head." He reflected on that statement for a moment. "Have you?"

Bolan sat. "If that had been the case I'd be on my way home by now."

"I guess so. So bring me up to date, Cooper."

"Matt."

Bolan related his involvement with the mob and with Clair Sorin—from day one up to the present. Sorin listened in silence, his only response being the occasional shake of his head.

"And how did Clair take it all?"

"She handled it just like Ethan Sorin's sister would."

"I can guess. She is great, that girl. But, God, it makes me so damned angry that they sent one of their thugs to her house. It's what we're up against, Matt. These bastards don't give a damn what they do. No respect. No conscience. And the OrgCrime unit has to work through channels. Held back by rules and regulations. We should be allowed to go straight for the throat. Fight fire with fire." He slumped back in his armchair. "But the idiots in charge rein us in, quoting legalese until our bloody heads spin. I swear sometimes I think they're all in bed with the crooks."

"From what I've learned, it sounds as if someone in your unit *is* working for the mob."

"There's a leak. We don't know who it is. So it's getting to the point where we're suspecting our own."

"That's what brought you up here?"

"My team, me included, were tired of all the crap we had to take. We felt useless. So the three of us decided to try something off the books. We had some intel on a mob house outside London. We came up with a plan and pushed it through. To be bloody honest, Matt, I don't think we really knew what we might find. But when we broke in, like a bunch of amateur thieves, we had luck on our side. There was only one bloke in the place. We tied him up and went looking for evidence. Turns out this guy was the mob's data operator. Silly sod didn't even have encryptions on his computer system. Schiller was our cyber expert. He got into the system and hit pure gold. Lists, reams of them, detailing names and locations, paid accounts. All the bastards the mob is paying off—lawyers, judges, cops. In the U.K., Europe and even the U.S. Names of suppliers. Delivery routes. Too much to detail right now, but it was a bloody find. First thing we did was load it onto a data stick and left before our luck ran out." Sorin shook his head. "But we made a mistake, Matt. We left a witness behind. The data operator. If the positions had been reversed the mob would have made sure there wasn't someone left behind to identify us. We didn't."

"Ethan, you couldn't have done anything else. You're not the mob. Killing in cold blood isn't in you."

"But that got my partners killed and has me on the run. All I can figure is the mob bloke must have got in touch with his people and they passed our descriptions on to the mole. Hell, I don't know, Matt. Maybe there was some concealed camera at that house we missed. Maybe we went at it unprepared. But the bastards got our descriptions. We decided to lay low after the mission. We'd gone against orders, so we knew we'd get hell when we went in. This leak in the unit had us wondering who to trust, so we decided to separate until things cooled down. Schiller went to his home in Germany. Larry Cobb had a bolt hole in Paris. I decided to come up here after I secured the data stick in a safe place. Larry Cobb called the day he was murdered. He must have realized they were coming for him. He told me Schiller had already been hit and not to trust anyone. I had the information we'd built up, so Larry told me to hide out until I could figure out how to get the information to someone trustworthy. I took his advice, and even then I nearly didn't make it. Someone showed up and tried to deal with me the minute I went to pick up my car. I caught his bullet in my side. Tore me up but didn't penetrate. I jumped him and we fought—I was lucky enough to put him down. Then I got to my car and got the hell out of there. It was almost dark and I was gone before anyone could spot me. I drove out of London, picked up the A1 heading north and just kept driving. I didn't stop for a couple of hours. I located a motor lodge and booked in. By then I was pretty weak. Bleeding had stopped. I took the first-aid kit out of the car and did what I could to clean and bandage the wound. Then I flaked out and slept. In the morning I had breakfast, bought a thermos flask from the lodge shop and had it filled with black coffee. After that I kept driving north. I survived on coffee refills and sheer bloody stubbornness. I wasn't going to let those buggers get to me. When I reached the village I stopped at the shop and stocked up on food and drink. Came here and you can see the result."

Sorin's shoulders slumped. "Selfish move," he said. "I should have thought about Clair. I just didn't think she might be in danger. If anything happens to her…"

"Ethan, you had enough to be dealing with."

A sudden spasm racked Sorin's body. His face showed a sheen of sweat as he clutched his side.

"Damned infection," he said. "Tried to hold it back but I don't have the stuff to deal with it."

"Then we'll have to make sure you get it. Ethan, I need to get you to a hospital."

"I know."

Bolan raised his head, listening. Above the wind he had picked up a faint, rising sound.

One he recognized.

One that was all too familiar.

The *thwack* of a helicopter's rotors coming toward the house. There was no mistaking the sound.

"You got your weapon handy?" Bolan asked.

Sorin nodded. He reached out and picked up the Glock handgun resting on the small table next to his armchair.

"I hear it now," he said. "Do we assume the worst?"

Bolan said, "Until we know different." He indicated the stairs. "I need a better observation spot."

Sorin watched him vanish up the stairs, heard Bolan's boots as he crossed the landing and made for one of the rooms.

Bolan peered through the front bedroom window. The chopper swung across the front of the house, hovering briefly before it moved to the side. He vacated the room and checked out the landing extension. There was a smaller window set in the end wall. Bolan saw the helicopter circle in and come to rest in the open a couple of hundred yards clear of the house. Three figures emerged from the aircraft, clad in hooded coats, carrying SMGs. They started to close in on the house. One separated and headed in the direction of the rear.

"Ethan, one's covering the rear," Bolan said as he returned to the ground floor. "Two look to be carrying SMGs."

Bolan slid the Beretta's selector to 3-round burst. Out the corner of his eye he saw Sorin check the Glock.

"Can you handle the rear?" Bolan said.

"Watch and learn," Sorin said.

He dragged himself out of the armchair and limped in the direction of the kitchen, leaning against the door frame. He braced the Glock in both hands, targeting the rear door itself.

Bolan faced the front door, standing to one side so as not to present himself as a direct target. The 93-R was aimed at the door.

The heavy kicks at the door heralded the arrival of their visitors.

The door swung open.

Bolan heard a voice yelling.

"Go. *Go, go, go…*"

16

Markus had the presence of mind to drop to a crouch as the door cleared the frame. His partner didn't. Pikey rushed the door, his SMG's muzzle tracking back and forth, seeking a target. It was a foolish move that cost him dearly.

He saw nothing but the shadowy interior of the room, his steps faltering as he realized his error. There was no chance to correct his move. Committed to the position he found himself in, Pikey swiveled his eyes left and right, searching.

When something moved on the periphery of his gaze it was far too late to do anything.

The jutting muzzle of an autopistol aimed at his head, held steady in the fist of the big American, was Pikey's last image. Bolan squeezed back on the 93-R's trigger and sent a 3-round burst of 9 mm slugs into Pikey's forehead, taking his skull apart and spraying bloody gore across the room.

Lapdog heard the subdued sound of suppressed gunfire, and then picked up the brief eruption of Pikey's final gasp over his comset.

In his shock and frustration, Lapdog forgot everything he had been told and let fly with his SMG, the long burst tearing ragged holes in the rear door around the lock area. Splinters spat back at him as the slugs ripped into the wood. Lapdog hurled himself forward, his lean shoulder smashing into the door. It crashed open, Lapdog following it over the step, his weapon thrust forward as he sprayed the kitchen with another burst. His slugs struck the walls and shelves, sending splintered crockery flying. Glass-fronted cabinets showered glittering shards through the air.

When his SMG snapped empty, Lapdog reached for a second magazine, his finger pressing the eject button to release the exhausted clip. It hit the tiled floor, bouncing. Lapdog began to slide in the fresh magazine.

And that was when Sorin showed himself at the inner door, his Glock 17 autopistol already raised in both hands. He triggered the pistol, his shots coring into Lapdog's chest, and followed the man down as he fell. Sorin's final shot struck the top of Lapdog's head as he slumped forward, the angled trajectory channeling the 9 mm slug through and out the back of Lapdog's skull. Lapdog toppled back, his upper body falling to the outside of the door where the rain washed his blood away in swirling pink streams.

Sorin, the effort taking the remaining strength from his body, sank to his knees and let his suddenly heavy weapon droop in his hands.

MARKUS CAUGHT A GLIMPSE of Pikey's head blowing apart. He didn't think any further than that before he wrenched his body aside, throwing himself away from the open door. He landed on his left shoulder, scrambling across the muddy ground, searching for cover. He knew Pikey's killer would be following. He was also convinced the shooter was the mystery American.

He just knew.

He rolled around the end wall, away from the front of the house, his mind working on how he could get clear. Markus understood he was on his own. Pikey was dead. And his call to Lapdog had not received a response. The burst of gunfire from the rear of the house had come from two guns, so Lapdog had engaged with a second shooter—Sorin? And presently there was only silence from the comset.

Jesus, what a mess, he thought.

It shouldn't have gone this way.

They should have shown up, taken Sorin and been back on the chopper already, free and clear.

Instead...

"ETHAN?"

"I'm okay."

"There's one more," Bolan said.

"Go."

MARKUS LOST HIS FOOTING and sprawled facedown on the wet ground. He almost let the SMG slip from his fingers as he pushed to his knees, his front slick with dark mud from his fall. As he stood upright he threw a quick glance over his shoulder.

No one in sight yet.

He didn't expect that to last for long.

Markus checked the area. There was nothing between himself and the waiting chopper except open ground—a rain-soaked field with no cover.

Nothing.

He spoke into his comset, alerting the pilot.

"What the hell is going on?" the pilot asked.

"Get that fucking chopper ready to lift off," Markus yelled. "Call Corrigan and tell him it's all blown to hell. They were waiting for us. Pikey and Lapdog are burned."

"Both of them? What about…"

"Just do it."

Markus caught movement at the corner of the house.

A tall figure clad all in black, thick hair plastered to his skull, stepped into view. There was actual menace in the way the guy moved. Markus felt a chill invade his body as he stared at the man. He had never backed away from a threat in his life but something about the big American froze Markus. It was more than simply his physical presence, though that in itself was intimidating. The guy exuded an aura of sheer domination. It was strong enough to make Markus hesitate. To render him immobile, even if only for a few seconds.

Markus shook himself free, aware he was allowing the man to put him under pressure. He raised the SMG, finger curling around the trigger, and he opened fire. The stream of 9 mm slugs pounded the stone wall of the house, sending a misty spray of dusty chips into the air.

"Sonofabitch!" he yelled as his burst missed its target by inches.

Markus pulled the muzzle around, lining up for a second burst. He stroked the trigger again and felt the SMG buck in his hands, wondering why the muzzle appeared to be aimed skyward. It was a second later when he registered the heavy numbness in his chest. The refusal of his lungs to function. Markus's ability to control his body left him as he toppled backward—explaining why he was firing his SMG at the sky. Pain took over then. Deep, wrenching pain that even dulled the sensation of hitting the ground. The impact drove bloody air from his lips. Markus was choking, unable even to draw breath because the 9 mm slugs from Bolan's 93-R had shattered ribs and shredded his lungs as they deformed and cored in through his body. He coughed up fragments of tissue, made an attempt to clutch his numbing chest but even that proved too much of an effort. Markus died with the looming figure of the tall man in black standing over him, his face impassive, the image slowly fading into misty darkness.

BOLAN PICKED UP THE rapidly increasing sound of the helicopter's rotors. The aircraft was powering up for flight. He was too far away to prevent it from taking off. He had to watch helplessly as the machine rose, turning quickly to remove it even farther from possible danger.

Damn, he thought.

The helicopter could have proven useful in transporting Sorin to a hospital.

Bolan didn't dwell on the loss. It had happened and no

amount of bitterness would change the fact. He turned and headed back in the direction of the house, reaching into his blacksuit pocket for his sat phone. He keyed in his Stony Man Farm number and waited as the connection was made. He spoke to Brognola.

"I found Ethan Sorin," Bolan said. "So did a hit team from the mob."

"You both okay?"

"Yeah. Ethan needs medical assistance. He has a wound that's turned septic. He should have that looked at ASAP. But we've got to keep him out of sight."

"A problem?"

"Can't risk the OrgCrime unit getting involved. They have a leak. Ethan has to stay covered until it's safe."

"You need my help?"

"Do I need to ask?"

"Hell, no," Brognola said, his tone gruff. "What do you want?"

"A pickup. Ethan taken to a secure location manned by *our* contacts only. Medical help."

"And kept under wraps for the duration."

"Along those lines."

Brognola chuckled. "Can you hang in there until help arrives? May take a little time. Give me your location."

Bolan quoted his GPS coordinates.

"Okay, got you."

"Keep me updated, Hal."

"Will do. Now get off the damn line so I can get to work, Striker."

Brognola's Stony Man position and his status within the Justice Department had garnered a long line of contacts. They stretched out from Washington and reached in diverse directions. His assets were spread across the globe and though he used them sparingly, Brognola worked on a reciprocating basis. In the ongoing struggle between good and evil, Brognola saw sense in agencies cooperating. Part of his work

ethic meant he stepped over the line on many occasions, loath-
ing the still-present reluctance of certain agencies to pool
knowledge. The stupidity of interagency rivalry left him baf-
fled. The western world was in a war, there was no arguing
there, so any withholding of information between people on
the same side simply aided the enemy. He wanted to get all
the heads of agencies in one room and personally crack their
skulls together until he drove some sense into them. It was
Brognola's fantasy. It rose into his conscious thoughts on oc-
casion, usually when he was frustrated.

His fantasy didn't surface as he picked up one of his tele-
phones and speed-dialed a number that put him through, via
a satellite link, to one of his U.K. assets. When his man came
on, Brognola dismissed the usual niceties and went straight
for the jugular.

BOLAN'S CELL BUZZED twenty minutes later.

"Three hours. Maybe less. They're on the way. Medical
assist and a ride for Ethan Sorin to a U.K. location. He'll be
safe, Striker."

"Thanks, Hal."

"I take it you won't be going with him?"

"Right there, pal."

"When the chopper arrives there'll be a package for you. I
figured you might be ready for ordnance top-up."

Bolan smiled. "You are not wrong."

"Stay hard, Striker. And alive."

The conversation ended. Bolan turned and gave Sorin a
thumbs-up.

"You'll be on your way soon, Ethan. Then it's time to turn
up the heat on the mob."

"One thing," Sorin said. "I need to let you know where I
put the data in case I don't make it."

"Okay, but you're going to make it, Ethan. I promised Clair
you would, and the last thing I want is to disappoint your
sister."

17

"Reese, do it. Hit the house now. Get that bitch. I don't care how many of those fucking OrgCrime agents you waste. Just do it."

Reese had his orders—and Corrigan's orders were never ignored. He pocketed the phone.

"We ready, boys?"

His six-man team nodded. They were all armed with SMGs and holstered handguns. Two of them carried sniper rifles. All their weapons were fitted with suppressors, and the entire team wore ski masks and gloves.

"Two agents at the rear. Same at the front. Plus three inside with the Sorin woman," Reese said. "We come in from the back of the house, take down the pair there. Then we split. One group in through the rear. The other round the side of the house and go for the two out front. We get rid of the agents inside and grab the woman. As soon as we have her, I call in the wheels and we leave. Minimum fuss. Minimum noise." Reese scanned the team. "Any questions? No? Let's do it, boys."

Reese had his team in the dense wood on the north side of the Sorin estate. The trees would give them good cover as they closed in on the house. The thick shrubbery and the orchard would help as they breached the perimeter of the large garden area. Once the patrolling OrgCrime agents at the rear had been dealt with, the final approach to the house would be clear.

The team was comprised of former military men Reese

had pulled in. He had worked with most of them before and trusted every one of them to do their job.

By the time the full team had assembled on the edge of the orchard, the forward pair had the OrgCrime agents spotted.

"One by the wall," Reese was told. "There. You see him?"

"Yes."

"Second is just moving this way across the patio. Near the steps."

"In range?"

"Of course."

The two with the rifles readied their weapons. They moved without haste, making sure their sighting was set for the distance before they focused in on the targets. The shots came within seconds of each other. Clean head shots. Reese saw the targets twist as the powerful bullets slammed home. Bone and flesh disintegrated, and bloody brain matter flew in misty sprays as the agents dropped.

"Go," Reese snapped.

The team sprinted forward, across the wide expanse of lawn. At the rear of the house they split into groups of three. Reese stayed with the team entering the house, while the other group skirted the side of the building, making for the front.

The wide French doors at the back of the house led into a large room, well-furnished, with a door that gave access to the rest of the house.

The team fanned out as they stepped through into the dining room. An agent in shirtsleeves was just entering the room. He saw the team and made a grab for the autopistol holstered on his hip. The rapid sound of suppressed fire hit him before he could clear the holster. He fell back against the door frame, eyes wide with shock. He was still falling to the floor as Reese and his team pushed by.

There was a sudden outburst of noise from outside the front door. The loud crack of a pistol, followed by the suppressed hiss of SMG fire.

"Move quickly," Reese ordered.

His team spread, weapons up and ready.

An armed man stepped into view, eyes searching for the source of the disturbance. He became aware of the team's presence. His upper body turned. He caught the unrestrained fire from two SMGs, the heavy bursts punching into his torso and blowing out his back. He was starting to bleed even as he fell, his hands clawing at the polished wood floor. Reese stood over him and punched a pair of 9 mm slugs through his skull, spreading a bloody mess across the floor.

The front door burst open and the other team crowded through. One of the men had a bloodied arm.

"Here," another of the men called.

In the library, where Delbert had missed his chance, was Clair Sorin, the surviving agent at her side. The agent was a red-haired young woman. She held a Glock pistol in her hand.

"Miss Sorin, you will come with us now," Reese said quietly.

Clair Sorin stared back at him. "And if I refuse?"

"The question does not arise. Does it?"

The young agent stepped forward. "What about my people?" she asked. "Are they…"

"Another wasted question," Reese said.

The pistol in his hand rose and he fired twice, his bullets coring in through the agent's forehead. They plowed through her brain and wrenched out a section of her skull as they exited.

"You bastard!" Clair screamed.

She moved faster than anyone might have expected, her right arm lashing out to deliver a wild punch at Reese. He barely avoided it as he leaned away. He used his own left hand to launch a heavy backhand that slammed across the side of Clair's face. She gasped in shock, falling to her knees, a bleeding gash in her cheek caused by the heavy silver ring Reese wore.

The only good thing, Clair thought, was that she had put her stable girl on extended paid leave since the protection team had moved in. If Jane had been on-site she would most likely have ended up dead, too.

"Bring her," Reese said. "Corrigan ordered she be delivered alive—he said nothing about any bruises."

He led the way through the house the way they had come in, across the garden and back through the wooded area. Reese used his phone to alert the vehicles and by the time they reached the pickup point, a pair of large SUVs were waiting on the narrow lane that ran parallel to the Benson home. Once everyone was inside, the two vehicles drove off.

Reese called Corrigan and told him they were on their way.

"Good. There were no problems?"

"Nothing to speak of. Cec has a bullet burn in his arm. Apart from that the operation was a success. The OrgCrime unit has seven less agents and will be realizing they can't beat us. And we have Sorin's sister to barter with."

"Time something went our way," Corrigan muttered. "You know what to do, Reese. Hey, don't let that woman out of your sight. If you lose her don't ever show your face again."

18

Tony Lowell had already flown in from New York and was settled in his London apartment, facing Corrigan from across the room.

"Christ, this a real mess," he said.

"You know how we deal with messes. We clean them up and move on."

"Not exactly happening at the moment."

"We've come through worse. It'll even out now we have Sorin's sister."

"Where is she now?" Lowell asked.

"Secure. On the boat."

"Heard anything from our *partners?*"

"Markel is whining all the time. And Frasko's been flexing his muscles—threatening to take over."

"I'm getting some flak from them, as well. Jesus, I'm pissed off with the whole damn thing. Having to stall them while we try to get those files back from Sorin is not doing my ulcer any favors," Lowell said.

"Which is why we need to concentrate on finding Sorin and getting that information back."

"I'm on it."

"Let's face it. Up to now it hasn't been entirely successful."

"I admit we've had a couple of setbacks."

"Jesus. Setbacks? Corrigan, I always like your sense of humor, but this ain't no fuckin' laughin' matter. If this gets out, you and me both are going down the crapper big-time. We'll have every one of those assholes gunning for us."

"Mr. Lowell, have I ever let you down? I'll get this sorted. My word on it. And when I give my word you know I'm good for it."

Lowell leaned back in his leather chair. He snapped his fingers and the armed minder standing at the side of the expansive apartment lounge immediately came forward to offer his employer a large cigar. When the cigar was burning well, Lowell waved his free hand, the heavy gold rings on his fingers catching the light.

"You want a cigar?" he asked.

Corrigan shook his head.

"Mr. Lowell, they are going to want a meet—I can feel it coming. They're starting to get real nervous. The Sorin thing was bad enough. Now we got this Yank in the mix. Bastard has caused us some aggravation and I don't think he's backing off anytime soon."

"What sucks is this guy seems to be some kind of phantom," Lowell said. "He comes and goes and no one can get a fuckin' line on him. What about your OrgCrime inside man?"

"Nothing. It would seem this guy doesn't have any connection with the task force."

"We have to do something, Corrigan. Make sure all our sites are protected. I want this bastard's head. And I want that goddam file Sorin has."

"He'll know by now we have his sister. And he'll have figured out that handing that file over to the OrgCrime unit means she gets dead very quickly." Corrigan smiled. "He's not going to part with it anytime soon."

Lowell bared his teeth in a hard sneer. "I wish I had your faith, Corrigan."

BOLAN GRIPPED THE WHEEL of the SUV hard. He peered beyond the glare of the headlights, seeing Clair Sorin staring back at him. The image was so clear it caught him off guard and he had to ease off the gas pedal. He forced himself to see the road ahead. After everything that had been done to protect Sorin and get him to safety, his sister had been taken. Henning's protection team had been slaughtered by the hit team.

Clair had been taken.

Was she hurt?

Injured in any way?

Bolan had taken a liking to the capable young woman. Her capture by the mob hung over him like a dark shadow because he knew these people—their vicious and unfeeling methods. The thought of Clair in their hands only added to his discomfort.

He had to get her back—alive. As much for his own sake as for hers.

He glanced at the SatNav. The bright screen was guiding him along a long road running through the Essex landscape. Here, the houses were set wide apart. The flat land offered little in the way of relief. He had already driven by large swathes of near-barren land. Industrial sites. Many deserted and dotted with tumbledown warehouses and workshops.

Joey Ballantine had given him a location for one of the mob's businesses. A site that handled stolen cars. In the isolated workshops vehicles were altered for resale. All high-end, expensive cars. Often they would be stripped down for serviceable parts to be shipped out to the mob's customers. Or details would be changed—plates and ownership papers.

"I only found out about this place a few days ago," Ballantine had said, "because there was a call out for extra heavies. The mob was looking for blokes handy with guns. I did a little digging. You, Mr. Cooper, have put the wind up the bastards. They're upping their protection because they don't know where you'll hit them next."

"I have a bad feeling about that," Bolan said.

"Only wish I could tell you where Corrigan hangs out, But no one knows where his personal place is. It's why I'm sending you to the place in Essex. Guy who runs it is Pete Kaman.

Story I heard is he's one of Corrigan's few buddies. He might know where Corrigan lives."

"Worth a visit," Bolan said. "Maybe I can get Kaman to talk. And shutting down the mob's outlet will be a bonus."

Presently, he was approaching the place. Slowing the SUV as the SatNav told him his turn was coming up, Bolan pulled off the road and onto a rutted dirt track. He swung into the shadows of thick undergrowth and parked. He shed his outer clothing to reveal his blacksuit and pulled on his combat harness, the 93-R rig and the Desert Eagle holstered at his hip.

There was enough light left to show him the layout of the sprawling workshop and the low-lying single-story house next to it. Bolan saw the stripped and rusting carcasses of derelict autos strewn around the area. Along with the old oil drums, and piles of discarded tires, it was enough to offer him cover as he moved in on the building.

Bolan met his first obstruction as he rounded the rear of a vehicle shell.

A stocky, wide-shouldered man in dark clothing, wielding a stubby mini-Uzi.

They locked eyes for a few seconds, then the guy went to lift his Uzi.

Bolan realized he had no time to pull his own weapon. Even in that moment he changed tack and brought his hands into play. Bolan caught the man's right wrist with his own left, fingers clamping down hard, twisting and pulling the gun hand across his body as he turned in toward the man. Bolan drove his right elbow up and slammed it into the shooter's face, hard. The man grunted under the solid impact. Bolan elbowed him a couple more times, feeling the man's head rock. He felt a warm spray of blood against his cheek. The shooter tried to free his gun hand but all he succeeded in doing was to jerk back on the trigger. The Uzi fired, the 9 mm slug clearing Bolan's body by a fraction. Turning fast, Bolan swung his opponent around and slammed him bodily against the metal auto body. The man's breath gusted from his lips in a bloody spray—Bolan's elbow smashes had crushed and torn his lips. Before the man could catch his breath Bolan slammed his fist into his exposed stomach—hard blows that hurt. A stifled groan burst from the guard's lips. He struggled to fight back but Bolan allowed him no leeway. He was aware the man was still holding his gun and any weapon in an enemy's hand was a threat. Pushing the gun hand down and away, Bolan used the moment to snatch the Desert Eagle from his hip holster. He jammed the big muzzle under the shooter's chin and pulled the trigger. The powerful .44 magnum slug blew the guy's head apart in a mushroom of bone and bloody brain matter.

As the bloody corpse slumped to the ground Bolan was already on the move. The shots would have warned the opposition. Any advantage Bolan might have had was wiped away, and his foray into enemy territory had been raised from soft probe to full contact. He was going to have to fight his way out if he wanted to remain in the game.

If he had been the kind who cursed his bad luck, Mack Bolan would have been in full voice, but that would have gone against his makeup. Long experience in combat situations had endowed Bolan with the ability to stay calm and use everything he could to his advantage. Melting into panic would get him killed very quickly. He understood his position and acted accordingly. He picked up the sound of raised voices nearby. Heard the scrape of boots on concrete, and figured there were two, three at the most. Bolan estimated they would burst into view within seconds. He flattened against the front wall of the house, the big Desert Eagle leveled and ready.

His guess had been correct.

Three armed guys came into sight, bunched close as they cleared the building. They were too close together to allow themselves firing clearance if they spotted their target. Bolan let them step into full view before *he* opened fire.

The Desert Eagle thundered in the close confines of the area. Bolan emptied the magazine, his calculated shots on track, sending the trio of would-be shooters down in a bloody tangle, their brief yells drowned by the crash of the heavy-caliber explosions.

Bolan jammed the Desert Eagle back into the holster and freed the 93-R, the selector set for triple bursts. He needed to maintain his pace—not give the opposition any stretch, allowing them to gather themselves. His sudden appearance had already disturbed their equilibrium. He had to keep up the mood.

He was hoping Pete Kaman hadn't been one of the men he'd taken down.

Bolan rounded the side of the house and saw a concrete patio in front of him. French doors were set in the house wall, and he spotted a number of metal patio chairs set around a table. Bolan reached out and snatched up one of the chairs. He swung it in a pendulum arc, releasing the chair and sent it crashing through the French doors. Glass shattered and wood splintered. Bolan followed the chair through, striding across the sill and into the room beyond.

It spread away from him, a bright room with scattered casual furniture and colored rugs on the tiled floor. On the far side, three wide steps led to a curving bar counter, glass shelves lined with bottles.

Bolan heard a voice yelling orders.

An armed figure, dressed in black shirt and pants, burst into view through an archway. He saw Bolan and raised his voice again.

"He's inside, Pete. Stay where you are."

The Beretta was already lined up on the guy and Bolan triggered a 3-round burst that spun him round and bounced him off the wall. The man slithered loosely to the floor, his face registering the shock of being shot. He flopped forward from the waist, his shirt starting to glisten red.

Bolan kept moving, pressing against the wall to the side of the arch as he heard the scuff of shoes in the passage beyond the arch. A shadow fell across the tiles.

"Hey, Jacko, what the hell…"

Bolan dropped to a crouch, the 93-R angling up so that when the man came into view, his bulk filling the opening, he presented an easy target. Bolan swung the muzzle of the autopistol up a fraction and placed a triple burst into the guy. The slugs burned in below the jaw, up through into the skull and exited in a gush of destruction. The shooter went up on his toes, finger pulling back in spasm on the trigger of his SMG. A long burst of slugs hit the ceiling, pockmarking the pristine white and raining a shower of dust on the floor beneath.

Bolan had eased around the swaying corpse before it fell, and was halfway along the passage as the dead man crumpled.

Since the house was on a single level Bolan didn't have stairs to worry about, just a complex of rooms leading off the main entrance hall. His only concern was the number of armed men he might be faced with.

Six down.

How many more to go?

Bolan paused, back to a wall, listening for movement that might offer insight into where the enemy was lurking.

Seconds slipped by.

Nothing.

Had he removed the team?

Was he alone?

He picked up the slight rustle of sound off to his left. Then the low creak of a door moving on dry hinges. Bolan focused on the door.

His question about being alone seemed to be premature.

Bolan watched as the dark ring of an SMG's muzzle crept around the edge of the door. The barrel of the weapon was being used to ease the door open. Bolan could make out the dark shape of the man holding the weapon. Then a hand, paler than the bulk of the body, gripping the fore section of the SMG. Bolan picked out the curve of the shooter's face, still partially hidden by the door frame. An eye moving back and forth as the guy sought to confirm Bolan's presence.

The guy was playing the caution card. Maybe aware of his

minders' earlier recklessness. More concerned with protecting his own skin.

And maybe because he was on his own.

That made him valuable to a degree, Bolan realized, for any information he might have.

So taking the man alive became priority.

The dead didn't talk.

Bolan moved the 93-R's selector to single shot. If he couldn't get the drop on the guy, he was going to need to go for a wounding shot. Bolan knew the odds would be longer, but if the guy refused a less-violent conclusion and tried to tough it out, Bolan would have no choice.

The door eased open a few more inches, allowing Bolan to see the potential target's right leg. He tracked the Beretta in.

"Step out. I won't kill you, Kaman," Bolan said. "Let me see the weapon on the floor. Your choice."

"You know me? So who are you?"

"The one you've been expecting, Kaman. Your people call me the Yank."

"Shit." Then the man said, "You expect me to roll over so easy?"

"Your buddies all took the hard way out. Left you to pick up the tab."

"Maybe I'm not on my own. Maybe I got backup in here."

"If that was so, you would be sending them out first. Guys like you let others do the dirty work for them."

"And maybe I can do it myself."

"I should let you think about that."

The guy did, but not for long. He made his play, which turned sour on him the moment he flung the door back and triggered the corridor with full auto-fire. Slugs hit the walls, shattered tiles and punctured the plaster. The overall effect was noisy but didn't cause any real damage.

On the tail end of his auto burst the man made his run for freedom, ducking low and breaking free from the open doorway.

Bolan saw the move, failing to understand the guy's motive. He didn't think about it for too long. The Beretta fixed on the chosen target, snapping out the single shot that caught the man in the right thigh and knocked him off his feet. He hit the hard tiled floor, the SMG leaving his grasp. When he landed, the left side of his face cracked against the floor, leaving him stunned and bleeding. He was barely conscious when Bolan kicked the SMG out of reach, and he offered little resistance when he was dragged along the corridor and into one of the rooms.

The shooter recovered some time later only to see he was in the kitchen, bound to a chair. He felt the heavy pulse of pain from his wounded leg. When he glanced down he saw that his pants leg had been cut away and a crude bandage was wrapped around his thigh. The cloth was soaked in blood. The side of his face, where it had hit the floor, burned with sharp pain, and he could feel dried blood on his flesh.

Movement caught his eye. He turned his head and saw the tall figure dressed in black, hung with weapons. The man's thick black hair framed a strong-featured face. The eyes were the feature that drew Kaman's attention—hard blue, like chips of ice. He was unable to see a trace of humanity reflected in them.

"You need to have that leg seen to," the man said. "I didn't hit anything vital but there's no guarantee infection won't set in. It's one of those things with bullet wounds even if they're not instantly fatal. The bullet penetrates and drags in dirt. Fragments of material. If it isn't correctly treated the wound can get nasty very fast." Bolan leaned against the edge of the heavy kitchen table, watching the man. "You're still bleeding under that bandage, too." He paused. "Anything you want to say?"

"Yeah. I need a doctor. You some kind of sadist?"

"I've been called a lot of things," Bolan said. "Never a sadist. What should I do about it?"

"Christ, you shot me. What do you want now?"

Bolan leaned forward. "A trade-off, Kaman. Your life for information."

"I should have fuckin' guessed it would be something like that."

"Play with the grown-ups, you get to pay the price."

Kaman stared up at Bolan. Sweat had sheened his pale face. He fought back a wave of nausea.

"You expect me to give up my people?"

"Don't pretend we're talking about a religious order. You're involved in drug- and people-trafficking. And don't forget the car-ring business out there. Your *people* are so low on the scale, I'm surprised you don't have to dig your way out just to see daylight."

"The hell with you. We run a business. We supply what's in demand."

Bolan's expression became bleak, his eyes colder—if that were possible.

"Have it your way. I'll get my information elsewhere." He holstered the Beretta and turned to leave.

"Hey, what about me?"

"What about you?"

"You walk away, I'll fucking die here."

"Not my problem," Bolan said. "You'd let one of your kidnapped women die if she became a liability. I've seen it happen. You treat them as if they don't matter. Human beings. Why should I show you any consideration?"

Kaman struggled against his bonds, teeth bared against the self-inflicted pain. Foul obscenities rolled from his lips.

Bolan had reached the door when the man yelled, "Wait. Don't leave...." He slumped, exhausted. "What do you need to know?"

"Just the address of Corrigan's apartment in town," Bolan said. He took out his cell and held it up. "The sooner you give me what I want, the quicker I call for help."

"I'm a dead man once I give it up."

Bolan shrugged. "Aren't we all," he said. "It's just a matter of *when*."

Kaman winced as pain coursed through his thigh. Sweat beaded his face.

"The address," Bolan repeated.

"Bastard," Kamen said, but he gave up the address.

Bolan made his call, bringing Henning up to speed. He gave his current position and advised of the need for medical help for the wounded man.

"Cooper, it's kill or cure with you," Henning said.

"I promised the guy help if he gave me information. He did, so now he's yours. You can go over the house, as well. See if there's anything you can use."

"Okay," Henning said. "Any update on Ethan?"

Bolan said, "He's still recovering. That bullet wound has left him weak."

"Has he been told about Clair?"

"No. The man has enough of a fight with his recovery. There will be time to tell him what's happened when he's stronger."

"Has he said anything about what happened before he went on the run?" Henning asked.

"I asked, but he wasn't in a fit state to talk. I'm just glad we got him back."

"Thanks to you, Cooper."

"Thank me when we have Clair back safely."

"Seems likely Ethan must have gotten his hands on something important if the mob had to snatch his sister," Henning said. "Damned if I know what, though."

"We'll find out soon enough," Bolan said.

He completed the call, then checked the guy tied to the chair. He was semiconscious. Bolan's binding of the wound had stopped the bleeding and would hold until Henning's team arrived with proper medical help. He told the bound man to stay still so he didn't start the bleeding again.

"Help's on the way," Bolan told him. "Hang in there."

"Do I have a choice?"

"Sure. Live or die. That's your choice."

Bolan made his way outside. He crossed to the vehicle workshop and pushed open the sliding doors. He knew what he was looking for. There was plenty of flammable liquid stacked up. It only took a few minutes to puncture drums and flood the floor. When Bolan exited the building flames were already starting to spread.

He cut through the grounds and returned to where he had left his SUV, changed back into civilian dress and drove off.

By the time he hit the road the workshop was well alight. It would be seen for miles, making it easy for Henning's team to locate it.

He felt no guilt at not revealing Sorin's information. It was the reason why the mob had mounted its search for his friend. But until he had Clair out of their hands, Bolan refused to come clean. As much as he wanted to place the information in the OrgCrime unit's hands Bolan held back. The crime force, as was its nature, would act on the incriminating evidence once they saw it. And if that happened prematurely, Clair's chances of survival would evaporate quickly.

There was also the problem of an insider feeding the mob. From Henning's admission the mole was still operating. Bolan was not going to pass along any data Sorin had in his possession until the OrgCrime unit had cleaned house. Two of its agents had been executed and Sorin was still under threat. Those deaths and Sorin's attack could have come via the leaked word of the insider.

Bolan had not forgotten how the protection team at Clair's house had been attacked. The mob had had exact knowledge of their numbers and had been able to hit quickly. Someone had passed information directly to them. That was another reason why Bolan had the mob in his sights. The attack at Clair's house had been swift and brutal, the killing of the protection team cold and calculated. The enemy here was ruthless. Brazen in their mindset that they were untouchable. Able to hit out at whoever they wanted to, wherever they desired.

Which was why Bolan was operating solo. He was under no obligation to obey the OrgCrime group rules. Despite their remit to bring down the mob, the constraints they operated under held them back from out-and-out hard-strike actions unless they had by-the-book evidence.

Bolan had no such restrictions. He worked to his own set of rules. He sought out his targets, pinpointed the guilty, went at them full-on and delivered the primal justice they deserved.

It was the only way to handle the guilty. They flaunted civilized laws, and carried out their evil with a contempt for anyone who stood against them. Yet they turned to the law when caught, using it to plead their case and quoting every precedent to allow them to walk away, surrounded by their expensive lawyers and smiling their way to freedom.

Bolan's law found them guilty and he exercised his own judgment. Courts and legal trickery did not come under his umbrella. In Bolan's world the truly guilty did not go unpunished.

In his court there was no appeal.

No bail.

All they had to look forward to was their execution.

Delivered in person by the Executioner.

19

The place was near Canary Wharf, but not part of that pristine redevelopment. The building was old-London in design and build. Substantial though, without the flash and glitter of the newer constructions that sparkled in the night.

Bolan cruised past the building and took the narrow street that ran down the west side. It was darker away from the streetlights and Bolan spotted a parking lot behind the place. He eased the SUV to a stop, climbed out and checked his weapons. The Beretta in its shoulder rig under his leather zip jacket. A razor-edged lock knife in a snug holster on his belt. In his pants pocket he carried a few coiled plastic ties. He had no identification, not even a cell phone. Bolan used the remote to lock the vehicle, then eased through the welcoming shadows and into the parking lot.

There were two cars parked up near the rear wall. Bolan caught a brief flicker of light as someone lit a cigarette. Keeping flat to the wall, he closed in on the rear of the building, picking up a low murmur of voices. He identified two of them.

Close enough he was able to make out the individual figures. Big guys, broad across the shoulders, shaved heads gleaming in the thin light fixed over a solid-looking door. One of the men turned and Bolan saw the silhouette of an SMG.

One guy made a low comment that brought a harsh chuckle from his partner.

"Well, I don't give a damn," another man said. "We should

be sitting up there in comfort. Not out here freezing our balls off."

"I'll call Corrigan and you can tell him that yourself."

"You think I got a bleedin' death wish?"

The man with the SMG laughed again, then said, "I'll go do another circuit. Stop me from seizing up."

He cradled the weapon under one arm as he moved off, fishing a packet of cigarettes from inside his coat. He went through the procedure of taking a cigarette from the pack, using a disposable lighter to fire it up. The actions kept his attention while he walked.

Bolan trailed him as he moved toward the far limit of the parking lot, letting the man stroll farther away from the light over the door. There was a blind spot at the far side of the lot—a shadowed area that would provide Bolan with the environment he needed.

His target paused, taking a long draw on his cigarette, savoring the taste of the tobacco. A small comfort during a night of boring sentry duty.

The guy seemed to sense rather than see a presence close by. He turned quickly. Not fast enough. The presence became a tall, dark shape that moved with a sound. And then something unyielding slammed across the side of his head. The blow was followed by another, second hit. The sentry felt himself falling, pain obviously flaring. He landed on his knees, hands thrown out to brace himself, but there was nothing to get hold of. He hit the ground, his senses slipping away. It all became too much and he slipped into a dark void.

Bolan slid the SMG to one side. He pulled plastic ties from his pocket and secured the unconscious man's wrists behind his back. Looped plastic around the ankles and tethered them tightly. He used the lock knife to slice off a long, wide strip from the guard's topcoat and used it to gag him. Satisfied the man was secure, Bolan picked up the SMG, checked it was ready for use and went after the second sentry.

He moved around the two parked cars, their bulk shielding him from the sentry. Bolan was able to close in on the man before he became aware of the Executioner's presence.

It was the hard prod of the Beretta against his spine that told the guard he was not alone. For a moment he may have thought it might be his partner having a joke, but the way the ring of steel pushed into his flesh changed that thought quickly.

Bolan reached around and slid his left hand inside the guy's jacket, feeling for a weapon. He found it in a shoulder rig. Bolan pulled the autopistol free. Using his free hand he dropped out the magazine and tossed the pistol over the roof of one of the parked cars. Then he threw the magazine across the car park where it clattered into a dark corner.

"Now I don't feel so intimidated," he said. "The next part is easy." Bolan had spotted the keypad on the wall beside the door. "You open the door and we go inside."

The man hesitated. "It's my job to prevent that from happening," he said grudgingly.

He was big, broad, and Bolan understood his tone. He had been caught out while doing his job and that would gnaw away at him. It would make him dangerous if he decided to attempt to right what he perceived as a wrong.

"We're changing that tonight. Now key in that code and quit stalling."

"You're that bloody Yank," the guy said.

"Then you'll understand I don't play around."

The man reached out to the keypad. "They want you bad," he said. "Corrigan wants to rip out your throat."

"I'm getting tired of hearing what Corrigan wants," Bolan said. "Now open the door before I put you down permanently."

The man tapped in numbers and the door clicked as it was released from the lock. Bolan prodded with the Beretta and the man hauled the door open. He led the way into a small entrance hall with a single elevator door. Without being told, the guard pressed the button and the elevator door slid open. Once they were inside, the button was pressed, the door closed and the elevator began its smooth ride.

"Anyone inside?" Bolan asked, using the Beretta as a prompt.

"Corrigan isn't here if that's what you mean."

"Right now he isn't my priority," Bolan said. "I'm looking for someone else."

"I didn't think you were offering subscriptions for *National Geographic,*" the man said drily.

"Move in front of me," Bolan said.

He had no intention of emerging from the elevator to a hostile greeting. The man was broad, with a solid torso and Bolan had no qualms over using him as a shield. He was dealing with lowlife criminals who traded in human life. Who sold drugs. So their survival was low on his list of priorities. If one of them got hurt during his entry to Corrigan's residence, so be it.

The elevator slowed and stopped. The door opened.

"Make it easy on yourself," Bolan said. "The place empty?"

"Except for the woman," the man said.

For a moment Bolan imagined he might be talking about Clair. Just as quickly his hope faded. His reason for coming here had been to try and locate Ethan's sister. He didn't imagine Corrigan would have left her alone in his apartment. It would have been impossible for Clair to have effected an escape given the setup, but Corrigan would not have risked even a slender chance for her to get away. If there was a woman here it wouldn't be Clair Sorin, so Bolan would have to be satisfied with information.

Bolan nudged the man forward. "Get over there and sit down," he said.

As the thug moved away from him, Bolan spotted a small wooden table with a potted cactus plant on top. He swept the plant aside, sending it crashing to the carpeted floor. Bolan picked up the table and placed it in the way of the elevator door as it began to close. With the upper door jammed, the elevator would not be accessible from below.

"Corrigan won't like that," a woman's voice said. "Locking him out of his own place and making a mess on his carpet."

Bolan looked around and saw a tall, attractive woman standing on the far side of the spacious room. She wore snug-fitting pants and a scarlet shirt. There was no hiding the supple shape the clothes covered. Shoulder-length ash-blond hair swayed as she crossed the room, pausing to rest one hip against the back of a large leather sofa. Her hazel eyes inspected Bolan from top to bottom, full red lips pouting in an amused smile.

"I'll just have to live with that," Bolan said.

"I recognize the accent," she said. "You must be…"

Bolan managed a weary smile. "Yeah, I know. The *Yank* who seems to be upsetting everyone lately."

"Do you have a name? It'll get tiring having to call you Yank all the time."

"Cooper," Bolan told her. He saw no reason why they shouldn't know who he was, because the name wouldn't gain them any advantage.

"Lauren," she said. "I'm the current inmate of this bloody place."

"By choice?" Bolan asked, intrigued at her use of words. "Or circumstance?"

She inclined her blond head. "I can't deny I walked in willingly, but once the bars appeared it was too late."

The tone in her voice explained a great deal. Bolan saw the pain in those hazel eyes and realized the woman was trapped in a world she couldn't escape. The luxury of the apartment might have shielded her from the outside world, but it did nothing to save her from the fact she was a prisoner.

"So what does he have on you?" Bolan asked.

Lauren's answer was to unbutton the scarlet shirt and slip it off. The fact she was naked beneath it only exposed the full extent of the still-healing bruises marking her white flesh. The marks were on her breasts as well as over her ribs. She turned around and showed Bolan the welts that crisscrossed her slim back. When she faced him again she held out her arms and Bolan saw the needle tracks there.

"He keeps me quiet by forcing the drugs on me," she said and her reserve broke, tears spilling from her eyes. "He does *things* to me, and when I try to resist…"

"Bitch, keep your fuckin' mouth shut," the minder yelled.

He had been sitting on an armchair, seemingly compliant. He pushed up off the chair and lunged at the woman, his big hand sweeping round to deliver a hard slap that caught her cheek. Lauren gasped, stumbling, losing her balance. As she fell her head caught the edge of a coffee table and she sprawled unconscious. Deciding he had an opportunity, the thug made an abrupt turn, coming at Bolan in a wild rush. He moved with surprising speed despite his heavy bulk. He threw out his arms, hands groping, and his right arm slammed against Bolan's gun hand, pushing the Beretta aside. The guy's full-on charge had a lot of power behind it and he drove Bolan back. A solid wall brought them to a sudden halt, the impact catching Bolan unprepared. He felt the man's hand clamp over his wrist, pushing the Beretta away. Bolan was no weakling but he quickly became aware of his opponent's strength. He launched a clenched left fist that connected with the man's heavy jaw, sliding across to the mouth. Bolan felt the jolt of the blow. He saw the minder's head turn from the impact and heard the expelled grunt. A bead of bright blood welled up on the man's lower lip. Bolan pulled his fist back and hit him again. Same force. Same point. This time the lips went back against the teeth that cut into soft flesh. The man swore loudly. He twisted at Bolan's right wrist, abruptly dragging his arm down and slammed Bolan's gun hand against a raised, heavily muscled thigh. Once. Twice. Bolan felt his grip on the 93-R slacken as his fingers numbed. A third smash and the Beretta slipped from Bolan's grasp, hitting the carpeted floor.

The big man spun Bolan around, clamping his muscular arms across the Executioner's chest and applied pressure, pinning Bolan's arms at his sides. His bear hug began to compress Bolan's ribs against his lungs. Bolan realized he had only a short time to retaliate before serious damage was done. His legs and feet were the only things free, so Bolan cleared the floor, slamming his feet against the wall. With his knees bent he had some leverage and he used it to thrust back, hard, and felt his opponent lose traction. Thrown off balance the big man began to topple. With Bolan on top, the pair went down. They hit the floor and Bolan snapped his head back on impact, the back of his skull impacting against the sentry's face, cracking against his right cheek with an audible sound. The big man gasped. He struggled to maintain his bear hug and managed until Bolan jerked his head back a second time, increasing the damage to the already injured cheek. The man let out a hurt roar, arms slackening, and Bolan pulled himself free and rolled away, coming to his knees. The sentry, clutching one hand to his splintered cheek, scrambled awkwardly upright. He was looking around for Bolan, who was on his opposite side, giving Bolan the opportunity to launch a brutal, hammerlike, double-fisted blow that connected with his target's jaw. The guy's head snapped round, blood spurting. He was flung sideways, hitting the floor on his left shoulder, and almost immediately his hand reached out for Bolan's fallen Beretta. Dazed as he was, the guy refused to quit.

Bolan's hand flipped open the sheath holding his lock knife. He slid the weapon free, flicking the blade open and launched himself across the floor.

The sentry's hand closed over the 93-R's butt, finger finding the trigger.

Bolan's right arm swept down, the steel blade of the lock knife piercing the man's wrist all the way through, shearing tendons and flesh. He screamed in pain. Blood was already spouting from the wound, spreading across the carpeted floor. The man's hand opened, fingers splaying out in response to the shock of the wound.

Leaning forward Bolan retrieved his Beretta. He brought his arm back, put the muzzle in line with the back of the man's head and hit him with a single tap. The man gave a convulsive jerk as the 9 mm slug burst his head open. Bolan placed a foot on the outstretched arm and pulled the lock knife free, wiped it on the dead man's coat and returned it to the sheath.

He holstered the Beretta and crossed to where Lauren lay. He turned her over. Her face was white. There was a blossoming bruise on her left cheek. Bolan scooped her up in his arms, carried her across to one of the large sofas and laid her on it. He picked up her discarded shirt and used it to cover Lauren's nakedness. He checked her pulse and found it strong and steady. She would come out of it.

He took a look around the spacious apartment. There was a lot of money invested in the décor—top-of-the-range furnishings, discreet lighting, expensive digital electronic music center, wall-mounted plasma television. There was also a huge, plain wood-and-aluminum desk, the surface clear. Bolan tried the drawers. He found little of interest. Nothing that might have given him any information regarding Clair Sorin. He had noticed the lack of any kind of computing equipment. No cell phones.

Corrigan, it appeared, was not the kind to leave anything lying around that might prove useful to anyone breaking in.

"Something suggests you're here for anything rather than just getting me out."

Bolan saw that Lauren had roused herself. She was on her feet. A little unsteady but upright. She was pulling on the shirt, fingers clumsy with the buttons.

"You okay?"

"I have the beginnings of one hell of a headache," she said, "but yes." She was trying to ignore the sight of the dead sentry but her gaze was drawn to the bloody mess his head had been reduced to. "Stupid question, but is he dead?"

"He kept pushing," Bolan said by way of explanation.

"And you refuse to be pushed."

Bolan didn't answer and she took that as a yes.

"Tell me why you're here, Cooper."

"I'm looking for someone these people have."

"Young woman? I recall Corrigan mentioning a Clair Sorin?"

Bolan nodded. "Do you have any idea where they might have her?"

"There's something at the back of my mind. Can't work it out yet. About a boat. Cooper, I want to help you. I just need to clear my mind."

"No pressure," Bolan said.

He wasn't about to push her despite the urgency of the situation. If Lauren had information about Clair it would have to come when she was ready to talk.

20

Lauren stared around the apartment. She went behind the desk and lifted a framed picture from the wall, revealing a built-in safe. She tapped in digits on the keypad and pulled open the door. Inside the small safe were blocks of banknotes. She took them out and tossed them on the desk.

"Corrigan isn't as smart as he believes," she said. "I wasn't always as out of it as he thought. And I have good eyesight. So I watched him open that safe and memorized the numbers. Now it's payback time. If I'm getting out of here… I am getting out, aren't I?" Bolan nodded. "Then I'm not leaving empty-handed."

"Go and get what you need," Bolan said. "We can't waste any more time."

She left the room to push open a door to one of the bedrooms. Bolan paced the apartment, frustrated that he hadn't come up with any more information. All he could hope was that Lauren might give him something useful when she remembered.

She reappeared, a large leather handbag in her hands. She had on a belted coat with a high, wraparound collar. She crossed to the desk and scooped the money from it into the bag, closing the zipper.

"Have bag, will travel," she announced. Her voice cracked as she said, "Please get me out of here, Cooper. I can't concentrate in this place."

Bolan led her toward the elevator.

She paused as they passed the wet bar. Bolan saw her swing the bag at the assorted bottles and glasses, smashing them to the floor.

"Make you feel better?"

"Closest I'm going to get right now," she said and followed him into the elevator.

Bolan kicked the obstruction away and let the door slide shut. He pressed the button to open it again and they stepped inside. Bolan hit the down button.

"Stay back when we reach bottom," he said, the Beretta in his hand again.

Bolan took his time when the elevator door opened. He was able to check the parking area. No more vehicles had shown up. The only difference was the rain slanting down from the dark sky.

"Keep on my left," Bolan said as he led the way across the concrete to the deserted street.

When they reached the parked SUV Bolan used his key to unlock it. Lauren climbed into the passenger side and Bolan started the engine. He drove away quietly, setting the SatNav for the M25. From previous visits to the U.K. Bolan recalled a large service area that had restaurants and a motor lodge. He needed somewhere anonymous where he and Lauren could talk.

Lauren lay back in her seat, the coat collar pulled up around her face, staring out through the rainy windshield. Bolan glanced across at her. Her eyes were open but from her expression Bolan didn't imagine she was seeing very much. He decided to leave her alone while he drove. In the aftermath of her experience with Corrigan she most likely had a lot on her mind. There would be a chance to speak to her once they were secure in the lodge.

The road was reasonably quiet and Bolan made it to their destination in three-quarters of an hour. He parked outside the lodge and grabbed his own holdall, made his way round to the passenger side and roused Lauren. She followed his lead as they went into the lodge. The reception was quiet, just one young girl behind the desk.

"Hi," Bolan said, his disarming smile putting the clerk at her ease. "Tell me you have a vacant room because we need to rest up. Been a long drive and we are bushed."

The girl glanced at Lauren who was leaning against the reception desk, eyes drooping. She had turned up the large, enveloping collar of her topcoat, hiding the bruise on her face.

"It *has* been a long drive," she repeated. "All I want now is a cup of coffee and a soft bed."

The girl smiled. "You're in luck. We have a couple of vacancies. Both double rooms."

Bolan had taken out his wallet and was extracting his credit card. He took the registration card the girl slid across to him and quickly filled it in. She completed the transaction with the credit card and passed it back. She barely glanced at the registration card before handing Bolan the room key card.

"Through the double doors," she said. "About halfway along the corridor. Breakfast served from 7:00 a.m. in the restaurant."

"We too late for any food now?" Bolan asked.

"I could have some sandwiches sent to your room."

"That would be fine. And a pot of fresh coffee. Double portions of everything," Bolan said pleasantly.

They pushed through the doors and along the corridor to the room. Bolan used the key card and got them inside. Without a word Lauren crossed to the bed and let herself down on it.

Bolan checked out the room, closed the blind over the window. A soft sound attracted his attention and he realized it was coming from Lauren. She was sobbing. He left her alone because he knew at that moment she needed to get it out of her system.

He tossed his jacket on a chair and went into the bathroom, turning on the cold tap so he could sluice water on his face. He leaned on the sink and stared at his reflection in the mirror, rubbing a hand across his stubbled cheeks. The face staring back at him looked tired. That was because he *was* tired. The last days had been hectic, fraught with the pressures of the mission he was on. Though he was reluctant to admit it, he needed rest, a time to recoup and charge his internal batteries. But Clair Sorin possibly didn't have time on her side. Wherever she was, she needed his presence before the mob decided that maybe she was too much trouble to keep alive.

Bolan didn't allow himself to be fooled into thinking Clair had an infinite amount of time ahead of her. The people who had her were violent and brutal. If they had ever possessed any kind of morals they had lost them a long time ago. If they had retained any semblance of humanity, they would not have been in the business they ran. They thought only about their own protection, and the profit they made from the operations they lorded over. Organized crime, in its various guises, traded on the suffering of innocents. These people did not give a damn about the hurt they heaped on their victims.

Clair was simply a tool to them. A pawn in the game they were indulging themselves in over the information Sorin possessed. And, like any tool, she could be discarded at a moment's notice.

Bolan had to keep that in his thoughts.

He sluiced more water over his face, then toweled it dry. He felt a little refreshed, but he needed sleep. And he decided he would get some once he had spoken to Lauren.

Back in the room he saw she was sitting up. Eyes slightly reddened, hair tangled.

"God, I must look a bloody fright," she said.

"No. You feel any better?" Bolan said.

"Sorry about going all girly on you."

"No apology needed. After what you've been through it's allowed."

"We need that talk," she said. Bolan nodded. "Let me get freshened up first. A hot shower's in order."

She dropped her coat on a chair and headed for the bathroom, kicking off her shoes. She stripped off her clothes as she walked to the bathroom. There was no kind of sexual provocation in her undressing. Simply a need to get out of her clothes. She pushed the bathroom door partway shut and moments later Bolan heard the rush of the shower being turned on.

Bolan longed to stretch out on the bed, but he held back because if he did lie down he knew he would be asleep in minutes. He busied himself checking the Beretta and feeding in a fresh magazine from his holdall. He did strip off the shoulder rig, placing the pistol under one of the pillows when he heard a knock on the door.

"Room service," someone answered when he asked who it was.

Bolan opened the door and a uniformed young man stepped inside, carrying a large tray that held the food and drink order. He placed the tray on the small table. Bolan fished a five-pound note from his wallet and gave it to the waiter.

"Thank you, sir. Anything else you need just call Room Service and ask for Jerry."

"Will do, Jerry, and thanks."

Bolan locked the door after the man left.

"Hot coffee," he called at the bathroom door.

"Okay," Lauren said. Bolan heard the shower turn off. "Hey, you want to pass me one of the bathrobes by the door?"

White robes, sealed in plastic, lay on the clothes unit by the door. Bolan picked one up and peeled off the plastic. He turned as Lauren came out of the bathroom, a large towel wrapped loosely around her body. She was drying her hair with a smaller towel. Bolan dropped the robe on the bed.

"What do you take with your coffee?" he asked.

"Tonight it's no cream or sugar. Just plain hot and black."

She dropped the large towel and pulled on the bathrobe, tossing her hair back from her face.

They gave themselves some time to relax, drinking the coffee and sampling the large plate of sandwiches, both of them aware of how hungry they were.

"Tell me how it happened," Bolan said. "About the drugs."

"Corrigan never overused the drugs," Lauren said. "Just enough to keep me subdued and expecting more. But the last few days he's had other things on his mind." She gave a wry smile. "I think that's down to you, Cooper. Since you showed up, Corrigan has spent so much time on the phone he almost forgot about me at times. Not that I'm complaining."

"What about the bruises?" Bolan asked.

"All part of Corrigan's charm. Something he enjoyed when he was having sex. I learned early on not to resist. The more I did, the rougher he got. Corrigan is not a nice person."

"How long were you with him?"

She smiled again. "A month too long. I guess it was my own fault. I fell in with a party crowd. We were having wild nights, sleeping all day. Just drinking and having fun. Corrigan kept showing up at every club we went to. Seemed to want to spend time with me and I fell for him." She refilled her coffee. "God, was I naive. I believed every word he uttered. Then one night after a meal out he invited me back to his place...." She paused, her eyes mirroring her bleak thoughts. "When I woke up the next morning I didn't even know where I was. I felt good though. Later Corrigan told me I was high because of the drugs he'd injected into me. I saw the needle mark on my arm and that was when the fun times turned into a nightmare. It didn't take long for me to figure out the rest. So I watched and listened to him and his people talking when I got the chance."

"So you know what they're involved with?"

"Drugs. Trafficking. Illicit goods. Big-time crime. I did hear about guns a couple of times. And I was there in the middle of it. Corrigan didn't seem to care that I heard it all. He kept telling me that when I was used up he was going to sell me on. I believed him, too. After a couple of weeks... I guess he was tiring of me...so he let his men..." Lauren fell silent, hiding her face in the big coffee cup.

Bolan didn't need her words. He understood what she had

gone through. It was not the first time he had heard such stories. He reached out to touch her shoulder.

"But you survived, Lauren, and there's no way you're going back there."

"The last few days they all left me alone. Even Corrigan." She looked at Bolan. "Someone was causing all kinds of problems for Corrigan. Someone they referred to as the *Yank*." She gave him a tired smile. "You, Mr. Cooper. Whatever you've been doing has rattled Corrigan's cage. So I played dumb and they forgot I was around until they wanted drinks-pouring or coffee-making. I was waiting for a chance to get out if it came up. But there was always someone around the apartment. No telephone. Corrigan always used the cell he carries with him."

"Couple of things I need to ask, Lauren."

She nodded. "This girl. Clair. Is she someone important to you?"

"Not in that way," Bolan said. "But she's important because Corrigan is using her to blackmail someone who has information he wants back. Clair's brother is part of an OrgCrime unit working to break up the mob. The information he has could seriously damage them. There's a possible mole in the OrgCrime task force. So we're in a tricky position. Clair is being used to try and force her brother's hand."

"And there I was believing I had all the problems." Lauren poured herself more coffee. "I hope there's plenty in that pot." She took a breath. "Okay, here's what I can remember. Corrigan did have a conversation via his cell with someone he called Tony. The name *Clair* came up a couple of times. Then Corrigan said he had her safe on *the boat*. He had a talk with someone about strengthening the crew on the boat in case you showed up. I managed to overhear him calling someone and telling them to get down to the coast and join the crew on board, getting Clair across to France. He was making a lot of calls around then. He got really crazy when someone called with some news. Obviously bad news."

"Hope he didn't take it out on you."

"No. He had too much going on even to think about me."
She touched his hand. "I have you to thank for distracting
him."

"All part of the service," Bolan said. "Lauren, the next part
is important. This boat. Did you hear a name? And do you
know where it's kept?"

Lauren stared at him. "Oh, yes," she said. "Corrigan called
it the *Venture.* I overheard him talking to the man Tony over
the phone. They berth it at a small channel port just up the
coast from Dover. It's called Sella Point."

Lauren poured more coffee. She circled the room, watching Bolan closely. Something was on her mind.

Then she said, "You're going down there, aren't you?"

"They won't come to me."

"Corrigan isn't going to be pleased at what you've done."

"His feelings don't matter, Lauren. He's on borrowed time.
And I have to find Clair."

She looked away for a moment. "I don't like to think about
that."

"In the morning we part company. You can stay on here if
you want until you decide what to do."

Lauren nodded. "Maybe."

"Do you have family you can go to?"

"Nobody. I've been on my own since I was twenty. Looked
after myself and did pretty well until...until Corrigan got his
hands on me."

"What about friends?"

"A few. But I won't be making contact until I know this
mess is all over. Last thing I need is to bring them to Corrigan's attention."

"Corrigan and his associates are going to have other things
to occupy themselves with."

"Maybe, Cooper, but I'm taking no risks. Without trying
to be showy I *can* take care of myself, the last few weeks not-
withstanding."

"I'm sure you can." Bolan wrote a phone number on the

small pad provided by the lodge. He handed it to Lauren. "Anything comes up you need help with, call this number. Friend of mine. Doug Henning. He'll help."

Lauren took the note and slipped it into her bag.

They finished their food and emptied the coffeepot.

"I'm tired," Lauren said.

"Take the bed," Bolan said.

"Oh, no," she said. "No sleeping on the couch for you. That bed is plenty big enough for the two of us and we're both over twenty-one. I'll take the left, you take the right. I promise I won't jump all over you during the night."

Bolan smiled. "I can think of worse things than that happening."

He left her to slip under the covers while he went into the bathroom and had a shower. He dried off, donned one of the courtesy bathrobes and eased himself into the bed. As he put out the light he heard Lauren sigh, the bed moving as she turned over. Just before he drifted into sleep he felt her wriggle closer and wrap one arm around his body. Her body curved against his. She was soft and warm. He agreed with his earlier statement that it certainly wasn't the worst thing that could happen to him.

When Bolan woke in the morning his watch told him it was just past eight o'clock. Sunlight shone behind the blind.

And Lauren was gone. Her side of the bed felt cold. Bolan sat up. There was a note propped up on the bedside table.

Thank you, Cooper. I won't forget what you did for me. Best night's sleep I've had in ages. I'll be fine. Lauren.

Bolan reread the note. He was sure the young woman would be fine. And he wished her the best.

21

Choppy gray water beyond the harbor. Heavy clouds drifting in toward the coast. There were only a few people around, which suited Bolan. He parked the SUV, made sure the Beretta was snug in its holster under the long coat and turned up the collar against the sea breeze—the air was cool and smelled of the sea. Bolan wore his combat blacksuit and boots under the coat, and carried his holdall with him.

There was a stationary refreshment stall situated on the quay, facing the harbor. Bolan strolled across and caught the eye of the guy serving. A beefy man with thinning hair and a red face, he wore a T-shirt that strained against his big stomach, and his exposed arms were tattooed from wrists to biceps.

"What can I get you, mate?"

"Black coffee," Bolan said.

The drink was served in a paper cup. It was viciously hot, steam curling from the dark brew.

"Quiet day," Bolan observed.

"Middle of the week," the man said. He wiped his large hands on a damp cloth. "Not much happening."

They spent a few minutes discussing weather and the decrease in business. The man seemed eager to talk. His quiet day left him with little to do except observe the comings and goings of the world.

"You know the *Venture?*" Bolan asked casually, watching for any adverse reaction.

"Nice boat," the man said, wiping the countertop with his cloth. "You looking for her?"

"Friend in town said to check her over. I need a charter."

"Thought the *Venture* was a private boat?"

"Sometimes runs the odd private charter I'm told."

"Well, you're in luck, mate. She's down at the end of the berth." He jerked a meaty thumb in the direction of the quay.

Bolan managed to finish the coffee. He dropped the empty cup in the trash bin and nodded to the guy. He picked up his holdall and moved on.

The sea breeze was bringing in spits of light rain, and Bolan was grateful for the heavy folds of his long coat. The quay was longer than he had expected and it took him a few minutes to reach the extreme end where the sixty-foot-long *Venture* rocked gently on the swell, her sides protected by buffers draped over the deck rails.

Bolan stood and checked out the motor cruiser. He didn't see any movement on the vessel. If there was anyone on board they must have been belowdecks.

He loosened the long coat so he could have easy access to the 93-R. His decision made, Bolan walked the final distance and stepped over the transom and onto the deck. He could feel it moving under his feet and balanced himself as he peered inside the main cabin.

"Who the fuck are you?"

Bolan saw a dark shape detach from the shadows inside the cabin. A lean man moved to stand in the open doorway. He was dressed in dark pants and a thick sweater. Had a shaved head above a scowling face. Bolan only gave these items a cursory glance. He was more interested in the MP-5 the thug was carrying. It hung from a webbing strap on his right shoulder.

"Wouldn't a fishing pole look more authentic?" Bolan said.

The man's scowl deepened. He took a step out of the cabin. "You making a joke?"

"Is Corrigan still on board? I need to talk with him."

"I don't know you, arsehole. Who told you about Corrigan being here?"

Bolan let the holdall drop to the deck. The distraction drew the man's gaze from his visitor. Only for a couple of heartbeats, but long enough for Bolan to clear the Beretta and place the muzzle against the man's forehead.

"You can't..."

The prod of the Beretta told the guy that Bolan *could*. He reached and took the MP-5 from the man's shoulder. Bolan draped it over his own shoulder then retrieved the holdall.

"Back inside," he said.

A look beyond the man showed Bolan there were no more occupants in the cabin. He maneuvered them both through the door. The interior was expensively furnished with polished wood and leather fittings.

"Sit."

The man did, still staring at Bolan with a murderous gleam in his eyes.

"Question time," Bolan said. "I get the answers I want, you keep breathing. And, yes, I'm that *Yank* who's been giving you boys the runaround. So you'll understand I'm serious."

The thug's expression betrayed his growing nervousness. Bolan had his attention.

"Corrigan?"

"He ain't here."

"Where is he?"

A slight hesitation until the Beretta was moved to center over his chest.

"Still over in France."

"Where the girl is? Clair Sorin?" The guy nodded. "Anyone else on board?" Bolan asked.

"Not any more. When Corrigan went across he kept the team with him. So there's just me, the skipper and his mate. They're in the wheelhouse."

"They armed?"

"No. All they do is sail the boat." A shrug. "I just take

orders. Not my business to ask why. Maybe there's more passengers to ship across."

Bolan backed up until he was pressed against the solid bulkhead. He placed the holdall at his side.

"Call your crew down here," he said. "I see anything that even looks like a gun, you're first. Understand?"

The man understood. Even so Bolan could sense his mind working, desperately seeking a way out of his current predicament.

"Do it," Bolan ordered.

"Calverton, I need you and Morgan down here. Now. Both of you."

The voice that came up from above the main cabin held a trace of irritation. "What do you want, Ketch?"

"I want your fat arses down here. Something you need to see."

The man stared at Bolan as if to say *What can I do?*

Grumbling voices preceded the appearance of Calverton and his mate. They came into view at the head of the companionway that allowed access to the cabin.

The *Venture*'s captain was lean and tanned. His eyes fixed on Ketch when he saw the man seated motionless. He didn't see Bolan, who was in the far corner of the cabin. Behind Calverton was a squat, bearded figure, holding a mug in one hand.

"What's so bloody desperate?" Calverton asked.

Bolan moved, attracting the captain's attention. "Me," he said. "Now go sit next to your buddy. Both of you."

"Who is this?" Calverton asked.

Ketch said, "The American Corrigan's been looking for."

"Are you serious?" Calverton said.

"Do I look like I'm about to start laughing?"

"Let me explain what's going to happen," Bolan said. "We cast off and you take us across the channel. Right to the spot where you delivered Clair Sorin. By the time we reach the French coast, I'll need to know where the girl is being held. Are we clear?"

"Just like that?" Calverton said. "As fucking easy as that?"

Bolan nodded. "Easy as that."

"This is crazy," Calverton said. "Corrigan…"

"Corrigan isn't in charge this time round. I am. Understand, my feelings toward you three are decidedly low. Stepping on you would be like crushing a bunch of cockroaches. You want to test that out, go ahead. Ketch first. Then the mate. Leaving you for last, Calverton."

Bolan allowed the following silence to stretch.

"Better do what he says," Ketch suggested.

"But—" Calverton protested.

"He has the gun," Ketch pointed out. "And do you know how many of our guys he's already killed?"

Calverton glanced across at Bolan. The expression on the tall American's face convinced the captain that the best thing was to do as he was told.

22

Still miles off the French coast, the weather had turned against them. The persistent drizzle became a heavy downpour, strong gales whipping the waves into a frenzy. The *Venture* bucked and rolled, dipping one moment, then rising to the sweeping crest of powerful waves the next. It was Calverton's skill at the helm that kept the boat moving forward. Along with Ketch and the mate, Morgan, Bolan kept a watchful eye on the situation from one corner of the bridge. He stood braced in a corner of the extensively equipped cabin, the Beretta in his hand a constant reminder he was serious about reaching France despite the weather conditions.

"How much longer?" Bolan asked.

Calverton maintained his watch through the main window as spray lashed at the thick Plexiglas, his hands busy at the helm.

"Hard to tell with this damn storm blowing up. It'll make our headway slow," he said. "What happens to Morgan and me when we arrive?"

"Nothing as far as I'm concerned," Bolan said. "Ketch will take me to where the girl is being held. So stay out of my way, I won't bother you."

Ketch, who had remained silent for most of the trip, turned to sneer at Bolan. "And if I tell you to go to hell and refuse to take you?"

"You risk getting shot," Bolan advised him, making it

simple to understand. "Choice is yours. Dead is dead. Everything ends for you. Figure it out, Ketch."

Over the next quarter of an hour the weather took a turn for the worse. Wind-driven waves hit the *Venture* from all sides. At times the vessel was surrounded by masses of roiling water threatening to engulf her. It was only Calverton's sure hand at the helm that guided the boat through the worst of the storm.

Even Bolan was finding it hard to maintain his stance. Pressed against the starboard bulkhead, he was forced to keep a close eye on both Ketch and Morgan. Calverton presented no threat—the man was too busy at the wheel to concern himself with Bolan.

The constant motion of the boat increased. The angle of the deck beneath Bolan's feet became extreme as *Venture* was hauled up and down the deep troughs. He grabbed one of the brass rails fixed to the bulkhead as the boat turned violently. Calverton gave with a shout of alarm, struggling with the wheel.

"Jesus!" he yelled.

The *Venture* dropped without warning, water crashing over the sides and seeming to bury the boat. The shock of the fall jarred Bolan's hand from the rail and he was thrown forward, close to losing his balance.

Morgan, off to Bolan's right, was thrown in the Executioner's direction, face taut with shock. He fell to his knees, arms in front of him and they collided. Bolan felt Morgan's hands clutch at his legs.

The moment was ripe for Ketch to take advantage, and he did. Staying upright by a superhuman effort, he hurled himself across the cabin. He slammed into Bolan, left hand gripping Bolan's gun arm, his right clenched into a hard fist that caught Bolan's jaw. With Morgan recovered enough to throw his efforts in with Ketch's, the three of them stumbled across the deck.

Bolan was banged hard up against the bulkhead. The impact drove breath from his lungs as he struggled to gain his freedom. Ketch was in no mind to let that happen. His forceful attack, aided by Morgan, gave him the advantage. They drove in a continuous barrage of blows to Bolan's face and body. And despite his refusal to quit, the Executioner was overwhelmed by the assault. Dazed, his face bloody and numb, Bolan was driven to his knees. Ketch gripped the 93-R and wrenched it from the big American's hand. He swung the Beretta in a vicious strike that connected with Bolan's skull, pitching him facedown on the deck.

"Go on," Morgan said. "Burn the fuck."

Ketch turned the 93-R away from Bolan's motionless figure, shaking his head.

"No," he said. "They want the bastard alive. And that's what they're going to get."

Morgan was disappointed. "I say kill the mother."

The Beretta angled in his direction. "Not your call—it's mine. And I aim to deliver this son of a bitch right into Corrigan's hands."

"Leave it, Morgan," Calverton called over his shoulder. "Ketch is right. They want Cooper alive. None of our business."

Morgan backed off, still dissatisfied, but knowing Calverton was right. The fate of the man called Cooper came under mob business and going against them could turn out to be fatal.

"Let's get this boat into harbor," Calverton said. "Sooner we can get him off loaded the better I'll feel."

Ketch said, "Find me a piece of rope so I can tie his hands."

He stripped off Bolan's long coat so he could search him thoroughly, removing the shoulder rig and the sheathed lock knife.

When Morgan returned with a length of rope Ketch bound Bolan's wrists together. He reached into his pocket and took out his sat phone, tapping in a number and waited for it to ring out. When it was answered, Corrigan's familiar tones snapping at him, Ketch grinned widely.

"Meet me at the harbor soon as you can," he said. "I'm bringing you a present. Name of Cooper. Not exactly kicking at this moment, but definitely alive, boss."

23

Corrigan's rage had been something to witness, Tony Lowell mused. When the man was told what had happened in London, he had exploded. He obviously took it very personally. The invasion of his apartment had been seen as an insult. The American had walked through his security team, breached the apartment and had left, along with the woman Corrigan had installed there. Someone had also cleaned out his safe, where he had kept backup cash. One sentry subdued and one dead. The *Yank,* as the elusive American had been named, was getting under Corrigan's skin like no one had ever done before.

The mob's heads had insisted on a meeting. Confidence in Corrigan's abilities had sunk to an all-time low, and a face-to-face gathering was demanded. The driving force behind the meeting was Lec Frasko. The aggressive Albanian was spoiling for a fight. He demanded a gathering at the mob's French headquarters, and, as he had the backing of the others, the decision was made.

Lowell found himself overruled. He championed Corrigan, but he could not in all honesty deny the others their say. He was disappointed in the U.K. failures, and the loss of men and product were facts he couldn't pass off easily. The OrgCrime unit had one of their people, Delbert, locked up. Corrigan vouched for the man's loyalty, but even he couldn't guarantee that. Nor could there be a valid excuse for the elimination of the team sent to Scotland to snatch Sorin.

Flying in to the meeting with his two top enforcers, Lowell stared out through the window of the Lear, deep in thought. He would defend Corrigan as much as he could. Yet he couldn't excuse the run of failures to the rest of the group—and Corrigan had accumulated too many errors over the past days to let slide.

The only saving grace on Corrigan's side was the successful hit on the home of Sorin's sister. The woman had been taken alive, and the OrgCrime team eliminated. So at least they had a bargaining chip to play.

Lowell himself had spoken with their man inside the OrgCrime unit. He had made it clear that he wanted Sorin told about his sister's kidnapping. The inside man had insisted he had no idea where Sorin was. The agent's protection was being handled by an unknown agency beyond OrgCrime's reach. Lowell had made it clear to the man that he wanted results. He reminded the man of his fragile position. After taking money and favors from the mob, it was time to prove his worth.

The task force agent's name was Tom Hanley.

"Just remember what we know about you and your family," Lowell had said to the man. *"That's just about everything. It wouldn't be a wise move to fail us now. Think about what you can lose—wife, children. You have an extremely pretty daughter. How old is she now? Yes, seventeen. How would you feel if we took her and included her in one of our auctions? You know the ones. I'm sure one of our Arab clients would pay good money for her. Young, white, blond hair. She would simply vanish and you would never see her again. That's just one example. Should I go on? No? I didn't fucking think so. Just do your job, Hanley."*

Lowell recalled the conversation with the man. He managed a bleak smile when he remembered the gasp of horror in the agent's voice at the mention of his family. Hanley had been so eager to collect his money and pass along information, but upon seeing the relationship he thought he had crumble with just a few choice words, Hanley had realized he was trapped. Trapped in the middle between the mob and the OrgCrime unit, with no way to turn. Lowell's hinted threats would hang over Hanley, shadowing every move he made. He might consider going to his superiors and confessing all, but it would end his career, possibly earn him jail time—and any relief he might feel would be short-lived. If Hanley crossed the mob there would never be an end to it. Hanley would never escape them. The mob had a long memory and it never forgave betrayal. Hanley's family would never realize it, but their lives would be forfeit sooner or later. If Hanley ever decided to confess, he would be handing out death sentences to his family.

The Lear touched down at a small private airfield in France. Formalities were nonexistent. The mob had long-standing arrangements with the local customs and the limousine waiting for Lowell was waved out the gate without a pause. He sat back in the deep, comfortable seat, his bodyguards sitting facing him, while the car sped along the road. It would take just under an hour to reach the meeting place. Rene Markel had already informed him the others were already there. They would want to commence business at once.

Lowell had no problem with that. He was anxious to proceed as quickly as possible. The sooner issues were resolved, the sooner he could get back to the States. Lowell did not enjoy trips that took him away from America. He preferred home ground. All this international dealing left him cold. Sure, he did business with these foreign partners because they had the goods he wanted, but he didn't particularly enjoy their company. He would take the money their enterprises collected. He would handle their goods. He would increase his business initiatives. But he didn't have to put up with their crap. He was Anthony "Tony" Lowell—an American, and a self-made man who had earned his bones long before his business partners started to throw their weight around. Deep down he didn't trust them, and he was sure they felt the same. But business was business. So the proprieties were observed.

Lowell stared out at the provincial French countryside. The rural scene did little for him. He was a city boy, born and bred. A New Yorker who loved the Big Apple. His early life had been lived on the mean streets—the feel of concrete beneath his feet, the noise and the smell of the neighborhoods all around him. His teen observations had made him appreciate the city's heart—the vibrations, the hustle and graft. His excursions into juvenile crime taught him the thrill of the game. Lowell graduated to the big time when he was nineteen after he made his first hit. He had done it as a favor for a local crime boss, stepping in when the hired shooter dropped the ball. From that day on Lowell became a made man. He learned to pay his respects to the bosses, to maintain a favorable attitude, and he watched and listened to everything that went on around him. His diligence paid off. By the time he was in his early twenties, with three more hits behind him, Lowell was in charge of his own team. His advancement had been steady—unspectacular but steady. Above all he was a trusted employee. In a dishonest profession, Lowell was a straight dealer. He understood the benefits of being honest to his crime family, and no one could ever accuse him of being underhanded. This brought its own rewards. People talked to him, knowing he would maintain a trust and never betray a confidence. He cultivated his informants and built a group of contacts both inside and outside the law. Life was good to him.

When a rival family had made an unexpected bid to take down the company Lowell was part of, there was a brief but bloody standoff. The takeover failed but not without cost on both sides. Lowell's boss and his top men died, as did over half of the rival family. There was a period of confusion—an empty chair to be filled. Lowell realized an opportunity and made his move, assuming control and easing his own people into the top positions. There was no opposition. No one who wanted the job. Lowell became the *Capo*. He made it clear that his intention was to run his crew and make no moves against any other mobs. He maintained his word, concentrating on his own businesses. He had always had a good eye for opportunities and the propositions he received from the European mobs interested him. Within a couple of years his ties with his extended family were bringing in unheard-of profits from the various enterprises they were dealing in.

The drugs coming in from Afghanistan meant he didn't need to become involved with the vicious Mexican and Colombian mobs.

The human cargoes from Frasko's highly organized Albanian connection provided women and girls from various European and U.S. locations. The volatile Frasko, a dedicated trader in people, was a hard man to deal with, but his goods were always top-grade.

There was also always a steady trade in weapons. Hans Coblenz, the humorless German, ran a complex of dealers that ranged across Europe. He had a solid connection within Russia where surplus weapons were still readily available, and Lowell had customers in the U.S. for some of those.

With the rest of the group, Lowell was part of a syndicate with multiple supply-and-demand branches.

With the formation of the OrgCrime task force, life had become less comfortable for a time. Though its intentions were serious, the OrgCrime group was hampered because it had to follow rules. Its legal division hammered it home to the multinational agencies that anything and everything they did must be legally sound. Rules and regulations. Human Rights. Legalese. It made the agencies almost powerless. The departments were swamped with paperwork and virtually strangled by the rule of law. Getting an inside man had been a bonus, and Hanley had proven his worth by feeding solid information to the mob. When he learned about the information theft carried out by three of the OrgCrime agents, Hanley had helped identify them. Two of the agents died. The third, Ethan Sorin, had eluded his killers so far and had gone into hiding.

That had been bad enough, but an added complication had arrived in the shape of the unknown American who had started to initiate hard strikes against the mob. No one, not even Hanley, had known anything about the Yank. It was only after Delbert's failed attempt against Sorin's sister that Hanley had learned the man's name.

Cooper.

It did them little good, though, because every attempt to learn more about him produced nothing. The guy was a ghost. A shadow who came and went at will, usually leaving a trail of broken bodies behind. Lowell gave the man credit for his ability to come and go like a wisp of smoke. But he wanted the bastard caught and put down before he destroyed the mob.

One man with the ability to create havoc wherever he showed. It would have been laughable if it hadn't been so damned serious. The whole mob seemingly powerless to stop a single man.

Even Corrigan was being made to look a fucking idiot, Lowell thought then. Which brought him back to the present and the rendezvous he was making with the rest of the group at the château the organization owned.

He felt the car slow a short time later. It turned off the narrow road, swept past stone columns and high iron gates. It approached the big house along a winding drive, through an avenue of tall trees, and Lowell studied the outline of the château that had stood in the grounds for more than two hundred and fifty years.

Lowell was not impressed. In his eyes it was an ugly pile. All crenellated stone and leaded windows. Seeing the place made him long for his New York apartment overlooking the Hudson. He hoped his visit here would be a short one so he could head back home soon.

The limousine stopped in line with the stone steps that led to the entrance. A number of other vehicles were already parked there.

"You want me to check first?"

Lowell glanced at his bodyguard.

"Frankie, if we can't trust our business partners, what the hell." Lowell grinned. "Do it anyway."

Frankie and the second minder, a blond-haired younger man called Leonard, eased out of the limousine and had a walk around the entrance area. Under the long, lightweight topcoats they each carried a 9 mm Uzi. The weapons were capable of rapid rates of fire and both men were skilled in their use.

Frankie moved to the door as it opened.

Rene Markel extended his arms in a welcoming gesture. He wore his dark hair to the collar of his expensive suit, underneath which was a thin, striped shirt and a dark tie. He was in his early forties, sleek and good-looking.

"It is good to see you, Tony," he said. "Even under these circumstances. *Vous-êtes les bienvenus, mon ami.*"

Lowell nodded. "Everyone here?"

"Yes."

Markel led the way inside. Lowell's bodyguards fell in close behind. The Frenchman guided them across the entrance hall and through a door that took them into a large, well furnished room.

Lowell recognized the five heads of the mob, each of them accompanied by their own bodyguards. He greeted each man in turn before taking his place at the head of the long oak table that had been readied for the meeting. As the heads sat down, the bodyguards took up positions behind their respective bosses.

"I wish we were meeting under better circumstances," Lowell said.

"This needs sorting," Frasko said. As usual he showed little patience. "And where is Corrigan? Has he decided to stay away from the mess he has created?"

"Let's keep this civilized, Lec," Lowell said. "No need to go off on one of your rants."

Frasko slapped his hands down on the table. "The hell with that," he said. "Your man has fucked up. No pretending he has not. I have lost money since this American showed up. I do not like to lose money."

The Italian, Astrianni, raised a placating hand. "We all have lost money," he said. His English was heavily accented. "That is not the most important consideration here."

Frasko laughed. "Only you could say that. I do all the work gathering the women so you can sit back and take the profit."

"You whine too much," Coblenz said. "Albanians are such a miserable breed."

"Kraut," Frasko snapped.

The German leaned forward, jabbing a thick finger at Frasko. "Peasant."

"Enough," Lowell yelled, half rising and pounding a fist on the table. "What the fuck is wrong with you people? We have a problem on our hands. No point arguing among ourselves. We need to fix this. Now keep quiet unless you have something useful to say."

Markel quietly cleared his throat. "*I* have something to report that might satisfy you all."

"Go ahead, Rene," Lowell said.

"I wanted to wait until we were all assembled. I received a call from Corrigan about twenty minutes ago. He is on his way from meeting the *Venture*. Which is why he is not here at the moment. He is bringing us an unexpected guest. Someone we have all been waiting to meet."

All heads turned in the Frenchman's direction.

"Rene?" Lowell asked.

"He is bringing in our mystery American. The man himself—Cooper. He is Corrigan's prisoner."

24

They were met at the small harbor. Waves were still slamming into the *Venture*'s hull when Calverton maneuvered the vessel through the harbor entrance, sheltered by stone walls from the fury of the English Channel. He brought the boat around and executed a by-the-book berthing. Morgan transferred to the quayside, hauling the mooring ropes into place fore and aft.

A full-size SUV was parked and waiting. Corrigan's imposing figure stood by the vehicle, ignoring the rain that still fell from cloud-heavy skies.

The moment the *Venture* was secure, Ketch appeared with Bolan, hands bound in front of him, being pushed across the deck. Ketch prodded his prisoner with the muzzle of the 93-R and Bolan stepped off the boat. Ketch carried Bolan's holdall in his free hand.

Corrigan moved to confront Bolan.

"Bienvenue en France," he said. "I guess you've had better welcomes."

Bolan met the man's taut stare, refusing to back down.

"Remember what you told me?" Ketch said. *"Dead is dead."*

Bolan turned to stare at the man. "I remember."

"Keep it in mind. Now move. I don't want to stand in the rain all damn day."

Bolan was put in the rear of the SUV. Corrigan took the Beretta from Ketch, who climbed behind the wheel, dumping Bolan's holdall in the passenger footwell. The big vehicle rolled across the quay and picked up the road beyond. As houses fell behind them, exposing empty countryside, Bolan settled in the soft leather seat.

"It'll take us about forty-five minutes," Corrigan said.

"I'm in no hurry," Bolan said.

"I should empty this fucking gun into you right now for what you've done."

Bolan's bloody lips etched a thin smile. "I did warn you."

"You cost us some good men, Cooper. Too many."

"First you have to define *good* men."

Corrigan shook his head. "You've got balls. I have to give you that. Let's forget the men you put down. Instead we'll talk about how you've made me look a damn fool in front of the people I work for."

It wasn't difficult, Bolan thought.

He kept the thought to himself. Bolan did not feel inclined to discuss Corrigan's embarrassment. He didn't give a damn about the man's feelings. Corrigan worked for the mob, which made him as guilty as they were. Right at that moment Bolan was mentally kicking himself for falling right into the mob's hands.

He was not feeling sorry for himself—it wasn't in Bolan's makeup to tolerate self-pity. That was self-defeating. Bolan remained positive. It was the only way out of a difficult situation, and right now he *was* in a difficult position. No doubt about that. He ached from a dozen sore spots on his body and face. Ketch and Morgan had been more than enthusiastic in their treatment of him back on the *Venture*. He was going to have several bruises on his body and his ribs down his left side gave him pain with every breath. His face was bloody and the gash in his scalp where Ketch had slugged him with the Beretta was still wet with blood. He also had his wrists tightly bound.

Ketch had tied his hands in front. He should have secured Bolan's hands behind him—it was an error Bolan wasn't about to point out. And it did present him with a degree of flexibility for later, but for the moment he was allowing his battered body to heal itself. Letting his strength build while he listened to Corrigan. As long as the man talked, he wasn't doing anything else to Bolan.

"You know what really makes me mad?" Corrigan said. "The fact that you broke into my apartment. Violated my personal space and left one of my boys dead."

"I called round but you were out. I was looking for Clair Sorin. Your guy forced my hand."

"You really are a direct bastard. Clair wasn't there so you played Mr. Gallant and took that bitch Lauren away instead."

"Seeing how you'd been treating her, it seemed the right thing to do."

"And my money?"

"Lauren figured you owed her. Have to give her the benefit of the doubt."

"I had a feeling she was sharper than she let on," Corrigan said. "But I had things on my mind at the time. If I ever get my hands on her again..."

"No," Bolan said. "She's long gone. Even I don't know where to."

Corrigan dismissed the subject with a wave of his hand.

"I want to know about you, Cooper. You're a nervy son of a bitch. You come out of nowhere and start chopping up my people. Taking away our merchandise. Just who are you? No one seems to be clued in to who you work for. So, what? Military SpecOps? SEAL? Some kind of Delta Force maverick? There's no way you belong to that pussy OrgCrime unit. All they do is run around like headless chickens waving paperwork at us. But you come storming in like some wild ass, shooting everybody on sight. What the hell set of rules do you work from?"

"My own," Bolan said. "Not hard to understand. I see a dirt bag, I take him down."

Corrigan smiled. "You should be working for me," he said.

"Not really. I'm fussy about the company I keep."

"And you like to push people's buttons. Be careful, Cooper, because I can lose it at any time."

"If you wanted me dead right now we wouldn't be discussing the meaning of life," Bolan said. "You would have told Ketch to shoot me and toss my body overboard while we were still in the Channel."

"He's fuckin' right there," Ketch said.

Corrigan appeared to have lost interest in the subject. He was examining the Beretta, working the forward hand lever, and checking the fire selector.

"Nice piece," he said. "This the one with 3-shot mode?"

Bolan nodded. "Handy when it comes to dealing with scum."

Corrigan refused to bite.

Conversation lapsed.

Over Corrigan's shoulder Bolan watched the French countryside go by in a blur. Ketch drove fast, with excellent control, the SUV going hard along a narrow country road. Bolan pushed himself into the corner of the seat, ignoring the pain that kept letting him know it was not going away. He flexed his muscles as much as he could without making it too obvious to Corrigan.

"Were you serious about wanting to break the mob up?" Corrigan asked.

"I don't joke about my intentions."

"How are you going to do it now?" Corrigan gestured with the 93-R. "You don't have much going for you at the moment."

At the moment maybe, Bolan internalized. *But things change.*

His response to Corrigan's comment was a slight shrug.

"Jesus, Cooper, you make it easy for a man to get angry with you."

"Corrigan, I'm not here to win a congeniality award. And making casual conversation isn't my thing." Bolan raised his bound hands. "We're not exactly soul mates, are we?"

"That is true. Cooper, I have a problem. Maybe you can help." Corrigan spoke in a calm, reasonable tone. "Sorin's sister is proving to be less than cooperative. Could be you might persuade her to change her mind."

"She has no idea where her brother is. When he was picked up in Scotland, the rescue team were separate from the OrgCrime unit. They took Ethan to a secure site even I don't know the location of," Bolan said.

"If that's true then we still have a problem. Sorin knows where the data we need is. Getting it back is priority. One way or another I intend to get my hands on it. Which brings me back to my dilemma. I have Clair. Now I have you. I want Ethan Sorin. And I want that information back in my hands."

"Your bosses must be sweating just thinking about what Ethan has on them and the mob."

"They understand what that information could do if it got into the wrong hands."

"From my perspective it would be the *right* hands."

Corrigan smiled as a thought struck him. "The truth is the bosses can't be exactly sure just how much information Sorin and his late accomplices actually downloaded. How deep they went into the database. It makes them uncomfortable. And desperate."

"That supposed to gain my sympathy?"

"Hell, no. Just be aware they're not going to be in a favorable state of mind where you're concerned. If they have a couple of their boys kick the crap out of you, it's because they want answers."

"I'll try and not hold it against them," Bolan said.

"Be there in a few minutes," Ketch said. "Hey, Cooper, you feel like wetting your pants go ahead. We'll understand."

THE SUV SWUNG OFF the road, between the stone pillars marking the entrance to the grounds of the château. It cruised along the drive and pulled up alongside the parked vehicles.

Corrigan stepped out, holding the Beretta on Bolan as he

climbed out. Ketch followed them to the front door, hauling Bolan's holdall with him. They crossed the hall and Ketch pushed open the door to the room where the mob's heads were waiting.

"Gentlemen," Corrigan said. "An early Christmas present."

He placed a hand in Bolan's back and pushed him forward.

Lowell caught Corrigan's eye and gave a slight nod. His man had redeemed himself as far as he was concerned.

He took a long look at the tall, black-haired man and had to admit that despite the battered and bloody appearance, the man named Cooper was impressive. Even as he stood before them, a captive amongst men who bore him nothing but ill will, he stood upright, his strong-featured face impassive. The expression in his eyes warned Lowell he was not a man to be taken lightly. Under a hostile gun, his hands bound, the American showed no outward sign of fear.

"You've had a good run, Cooper," Lowell said. "Cost us a great deal. But it's over now, son. Don't believe otherwise."

Bolan stayed silent.

"Does he not speak?" Astrianni said. "Is he mute?"

"He can talk," Corrigan said. "When he figures it's worth-while."

Lec Frasko stood up, the force of his rising tipping his chair back. He stormed around the table, his face tight with anger.

"This bastard owes me for a consignment of top-grade merchandise. I'll make him talk."

"Lec," Lowell shouted.

"Go to hell," Frasko screamed, spittle spraying from his lips as he rushed at Bolan. "We have waited long enough."

Corrigan stepped back a couple of feet, keeping the Beretta trained on Bolan.

Frasko rounded the end of the table. His face was flushed with rage, fists bunched. He almost lost his balance as his shoes slipped on the polished wood floor. In his haste he launched a badly timed fist at Bolan. Grunting from the effort he tried to regain his balance. He was too slow. Bolan had swayed away from the intended blow. He pulled his own bound fists up and almost leisurely clubbed Frasko across the mouth. The sound of the blow was loud in the hushed room. Frasko gave a pained grunt and dropped to his knees. He stayed there, blood starting to drip heavily from split lips. Bolan moved away from him, hands dropping into a non-threatening position.

Lowell gestured at Frasko's bodyguards and they moved forward to help their boss back on his feet. Frasko was too dazed to resist as he was returned to his seat. One of them produced a large white handkerchief from his jacket and pressed it into Frasko's hand so he could stem the blood flow.

"He isn't going to thank you for that," Corrigan said softly.

"I'm just disappointed you didn't shoot him for me," Bolan said.

"Hell, he's one of the guys who signs my paychecks."

Lowell raised his hands to quiet the murmur of voices around the table.

"Let's come to order," he said. "Believe me, I have no love for this man. But knocking him senseless right now isn't in our interests. This man has had contact with Ethan Sorin and his sister. We need to use that in order to get back the information Sorin stole."

"He claims he has no idea where Sorin is right now," Corrigan said. "The OrgCrime unit doesn't have him. Some outside agency pulled him out of Scotland and has him hidden away."

"Why should we believe that?" Hans Coblenz said.

"Because you have a man inside the OrgCrime unit," Bolan said. "Sorin's whereabouts fed to the unit would have come straight to you. His safety would have been jeopardized."

Rene Markel said, "From a security position it was a wise move."

"We can work around it," Corrigan said. "Now we have Cooper and the girl. As long as we do, Sorin isn't going to hand over his information. He knows if he does, his sister is dead."

"Your logic has a slight flaw," Markel pointed out. "If Sorin is being held incommunicado, how do we get the message to him?"

"We have our way in," Lowell said. "Cooper will come across."

"You think?" Bolan said.

"Every man in this room has the urge to kill you," Lowell said. "The only thing keeping that from happening is your knowing where Sorin is. We have the girl, and I have a feeling she might be your weak spot. We took her as a lever against Sorin. But now we will use *her* to persuade you to give him up. Simple arithmetic, Cooper. The girl. Sorin. You. Figure it out. If we don't get the cooperation we require, Ethan Sorin will lose his sister." Lowell caught Corrigan's eye. "Put him with the girl. Let him see her. Talk to her. Mr. Cooper might be the ice man, but I think seeing the girl will thaw him out."

Corrigan nudged Bolan with the Beretta. "Let's go, hotshot." He looked across to where Frasko, still holding the handkerchief to his bleeding mouth, was glaring at Bolan with hate-filled eyes. "You certainly didn't make a fan of him there."

Bolan didn't respond. He walked out of the room, with Corrigan behind him and Ketch to one side. Across the hall and up the wide staircase to an upper landing, then a sharp turn to another flight of stairs.

"Take the right passage," Corrigan said.

There was an armed man lounging on a chair outside a solid wood door. When Corrigan gestured, the guard took a key from his pocket and unlocked the door.

"I just love a reunion," Ketch whispered as Bolan moved by.

"Just don't take too long about it," Corrigan said, pushing Bolan into the room.

The door closed with a heavy thud. The key turned in the lock.

And Bolan found himself face-to-face with Clair Sorin.

25

"Of all the people I might have expected to see here," she said, "you're the most unlikely."

"That could hurt my feelings if I took it the wrong way."

Clair crossed the room and flung her arms around his neck, gripping him tightly. She seemed to notice his bruised face and stepped back.

"God, what have they done to you?" A soft hand touched his cheek. "Why?"

"Must have been something I said."

"That's just the sort of thing Ethan would say."

She busied herself loosening the knots on the rope around Bolan's wrists. He noticed she was wearing exactly the same outfit she'd had on the last time he saw her. Roll-neck sweater, jodhpurs and riding boots. They looked a lot less neat but Bolan wasn't about to complain. When she finally released the expertly fastened knots and pulled the rope free, Bolan felt his restricted circulation starting to flow again. He flexed his hands. His wrists showed raw marks where the coarse rope had bitten into the flesh.

"Tell me about Ethan. Did you find him?"

"Yeah. He was hurt, but I got him transferred to a secure place."

"Badly hurt?"

"Bullet wound that got infected."

Clair's face blanched. "Is he going to be all right?"

Bolan nodded as he moved around the room, checking it out. Apart from a mattress and blankets on the wood floor, the room was devoid of furniture. There were two windows, tall frames with leaded-glass panes. The heavy wood frames were screwed down. Bolan glanced up at the high, vaulted ceiling. He was looking for any signs of cameras and microphones. There was nothing to indicate any listening devices on the smooth walls.

What the hell, he thought, *if they want to listen in they aren't going to get anything useful.*

"You must have heard what happened at my house?"

"Yes."

"They murdered all the agents. Even the woman. She was standing right beside me when they…" Clair shook her head. "Matt, I don't understand these people. What's wrong with them? They kill without thought. Even wild animals don't slaughter their own kind like these do."

"They have no conscience," Bolan said. "Mindless thugs who don't give a damn. Expect the worst from them and they'll take it a step further."

"What happens now? To us?"

"They still want the information Ethan took from them. It's important they get it back. I'm not going to lie to you, Clair. If we don't give them Ethan's location and access to the information they *will* kill us. They put me in here so I can persuade you to cooperate. We give up Ethan and we survive."

"I don't believe that," she said. "Do you?"

"That's what they want us to think. With the information in their hands we become surplus to requirements."

"Well, that's encouraging."

"At some point they might need you to communicate with Ethan. Convince him you're still unhurt. Proof they do have you."

"Nice to be told I'm useful for something," Clair said drily.

"They'll keep us alive as long as we make them happy."

"But either way we die in the end. Some choice, Mr. Cooper."

Bolan drew her close and said softly, "Only if we stay around."

He cautioned Clair to speak quietly. "From what I saw before they put me here, everyone has a gun. And there are more of them than us," she murmured.

"Then we need to reduce the odds."

"Why do I not like the sound of that?"

Bolan said, "Do they bring you food and drink?"

"Yes. And take me to the bathroom at the end of the passage. Why?"

"How many bring your meals?"

"One carries a tray. Second man carries a big gun."

"Do they leave the door open while they're in the room?"

Clair nodded. "Are you…"

"Our best chance. As long as the door is locked we can't do anything."

She repeated herself. "Matt, are you trying to get yourself shot?"

"That's the part I want to avoid. If anyone comes in, follow my lead, but try not to get in my way."

No one came for some time—close to a couple of hours. Light faded outside the windows. They sat on the floor, backs against the wall. Clair moved close to Bolan, seeming to want him near her. Being as high as they were in the château, no sound reached them from downstairs.

"Do you think they're deciding what to do with us?"

"Could be."

"I can't believe how my life has changed. I mean, look at me. A prisoner in a French château. People wanting to hurt me. For heaven's sake, Matt Cooper, I run a bloody riding stable in Buckinghamshire. I'm not a female James Bond."

Bolan had to smile at her righteous anger. He could understand it. She had been torn from her normal, peaceful environment and dropped feetfirst in the middle of killing and sudden death. He admired her resolve not to fall to pieces. Many people, in similar circumstances would have. Clair Sorin seemed to be simply getting annoyed. He hoped she stayed that way.

Bolan had just glanced at his watch—it was close to eight in the evening—when he heard sounds on the other side of their locked door. Then the murmur of voices.

Beside him Clair stirred out of a light doze.

"What is it?"

"Visitors," Bolan said.

He pushed to his feet and crossed the room, Clair following him. They faced the door as someone inserted the key and turned it.

"Stay to one side," Bolan said.

The door swung wide.

An armed figure stepped inside. He carried an MP-5 SMG. The weapon was pointing at Bolan. It was the door guard.

A second figure carried a wooden tray holding food and drink.

Behind him was a familiar face.

Lec Frasko. His lips were swollen and looked painful. At his side was one of his bodyguards. The minder's jacket was off and Bolan could see he was carrying a 9 mm Heckler & Koch pistol in a holster on his left hip, butt forward for a cross-draw.

"I wanted to see if you were comfortable," Frasko said in his heavily accented English. He attempted a smile but pain from his split lips cancelled that out quickly.

The hell you did, Bolan thought.

"I had to promise not to shoot you," Frasko went on. "Don't worry. That *will* come just later."

"We were just wondering about that," Bolan said, his conversation generating interest. It was what he wanted. A sliver of relaxation on the part of the opposition—enough to give him his window of opportunity.

"Yes," Clair joined in. "Just how much longer are we going

to have to wait?" She injected enough inflection in her voice
to draw attention.

Bolan saw the guy with the H&K glance at her, a slight
sneer starting to curl his lips.

Now.

It isn't going to get any better.

Bolan twisted, slicing his left elbow round to slam into
the guy's face. The man gave a harsh grunt as his cheek collapsed from the blow. He stumbled back and Bolan continued his turn, snatching at the SMG. He jerked it free, aware
that Frasko's bodyguard was reaching for his handgun. Bolan
dropped to a crouch, lowering his body mass, and tracked the
muzzle of the MP-5, finger already at the trigger. He eased
it back and laid a short burst into the bodyguard. The man
grunted as the 9 mm slugs shattered his ribs, the short range
letting the shots tear through and blow out to one side of his
spine. As the minder dropped back against the wall, Bolan
caught movement on the periphery of his vision and saw the
tray bearer throw his burden aside and sweep his hand to the
autopistol tucked under his belt. The tray was still falling
when Bolan triggered the SMG, stitching the man down his
side, opening him up like pulped fruit. Bolan angled the H&K
and hit the guy he'd punched in the cheek. The burst took the
man in the throat. He tumbled to the floor, hands gripping his
torn, bloody flesh. During the initial seconds of the confron-
tation, Frasko had reached under his jacket for his own holstered weapon, fingers fumbling for the checkered grips of his
pistol. He knew he wasn't going to make it when his weapon
resisted his pull, tangling with the lining of his coat. Bolan's
borrowed weapon traversed under his steady grip. He held a
microsecond's contact with Frasko's wide-eyed stare of utter
fear before he punched out a burst that collapsed the Albanian's face and lifted the front of his skull in a bloody mess.

"Clair, pick up the handguns," Bolan snapped. He didn't
want her freezing in shock at what had just happened. "See if

they have spare magazines in their pockets. Do it fast before they start coming up the stairs for us."

He turned and crouched by the man he'd relieved of his MP-5. He found a spare 30-round magazine and slid it into a pocket. The man didn't have a handgun. Bolan picked up the food-delivery man's pistol, a SIG, and tucked it in his belt. An extra magazine went into another pocket.

"Two pistols," Clair said as Bolan faced her. "Just one extra magazine from the bodyguard."

Her face was pale, drained. She kept blowing out sharp breaths to calm herself.

"Can you handle a pistol?" Bolan asked as he led the way out of the room and along the passage.

"Ethan and I used to practice target shooting sometimes," she said.

"Required skill for an English lady?"

She managed a croaky laugh. "Hardly," she said. "But in my rebellious younger days I did roll my own cigarettes."

"Keep hold of those pistols," Bolan said. "Use them if you have to."

At the end of the passage Bolan paused at the head of the stairs. He could hear raised voices. The thud of boots.

Close behind him Clair said, "How do we get out of this one?"

Bolan didn't answer. He had seen cautious movement at the base of the stairs. Watched as armed figures filtered around the curve. He stayed behind the protection of the wall end. Clair's breathing was still ragged as she regained her composure.

Two men, SMGs in their hands, slid into view—one covering as the other started to edge up the stairs.

Bolan tracked the H&K on the guy doing the covering. He sent a short burst that chunked into the side of the target's skull and sprayed bloody brain matter on the wall. The man moving up the stairs froze. He was totally exposed. Bolan held him in his sights for a heartbeat, then knocked him back down the stairs with a hit to the chest that splintered bone and punctured heart and lungs.

That would make the others pause before they launched another strike. Bolan leaned against the wall. The reverse side of the coin meant he and Clair were prevented from getting down the stairs.

A stalemate.

He glanced at the young woman. She had one pistol in her hand, the second thrust into her jodhpurs.

"One of us needs to check out the rooms on this floor," Bolan said. "See if there's any way out."

"I guess that's me," Clair said.

"Can you handle it?"

"Looks like we'll find out," she said.

She moved down the passage to the doors beyond the room where she had been held.

There were three doors to check.

"Nothing," she said on her return. "All empty. One toilet. Windows all screwed down. I'll check the rooms on the other side of the landing."

Bolan nodded. He was watching the stairs. Nothing had moved since the initial attack. They would be planning fresh moves because he had left them no choice. Resistance *would* come. Bolan laid the spare MP5 magazine on the floor close by and checked the SIG. The pistol held a full magazine. Not as much firepower as he could have done with, he wasn't in a position to complain.

The lights on the lower landing went out, leaving it in shadow. Bolan waited, anticipating another move with the stairs in semidarkness.

He tried to figure out how they would mount their attack.

A full assault?

Or just a couple of shooters?

He got his answer moments later when autofire from a number of weapons shattered the silence. The fire was directed at the head of the stairs, slugs slamming into the wall behind Bolan. They were aiming high. It only took a couple of seconds for Bolan to work out why. The gunfire was intended to keep him occupied while more of the shooters made another sortie, moving beneath the deliberately high-angled fire.

Smart strategy, he thought. *Pity it didn't work, Corrigan.*

Staying low himself, Bolan pushed the MP-5 forward and triggered a long burst that was angled down the stairwell at the dark figures edging in his direction. The withering blast hit flesh and bone, drawing pained yells and screams. Stray slugs splintered wood from the steps, filling the air with stinging chips. Bolan heard the hard thud of bodies rolling back down the stairs. He ran the MP-5's magazine until it was empty, then ejected it and snapped in the reserve clip.

In the silence that followed, broken by low moans and one whimpering cry, Bolan heard footsteps retreated down the lower stairs.

From the passage to his right he heard Clair's soft voice.

"You have to see what I've found, Matt."

"If it isn't a mini-helicopter to fly us out I'm not really interested."

26

Clair moved to the head of the stairs to keep watch, leaving Bolan to check out the two rooms she had opened. They were on the left side of the passage. Large, high-ceilinged rooms. As Bolan reached the first room he saw a single, heavy door set in the passage's end wall. He spotted the steel bolts fixed top and bottom and made a note to have a closer look.

He turned to inspect the first of the opened rooms. It took a moment for him to register what he was looking at—plastic-wrapped blocks, at least four feet square, holding bundles of bank notes. They half-filled the room. Bolan couldn't imagine how much cash that would total.

"You see it?" Clair called.

"I can barely believe it," Bolan said back.

"Check the other room."

Same size room. Also packed, this time with stacks of wrapped drugs—white powder, brown tablets of unrefined heroin and more bags holding thousands of pills. Bolan scanned the room. A massive stash of narcotics ready for distribution. Enough to bring in more millions for the mob—and misery for the users.

He caught a glimpse of boxes stacked against the wall opposite the door. Familiar shapes and sizes. Ordnance. Bolan inspected the piled cases. Recognized handguns, MP-5 SMGs, and a container holding M-67 U.S. hand grenades. The markings on the box were U.S. Military. Bolan unearthed a box of

9 mm cartridges. A supply of magazines for the MP-5, next to a case of the H&K weapons. He took a half dozen of the magazines from the ammunition box, then tucked one of the MP-5s under his arm and returned to where Clair crouched.

"Any movement?"

She shook her head. "I heard voices. Nothing else."

Bolan opened the ammunition box and laid out the empty magazines, then began to load the mags. Clair watched him for a while, then took one of the mags and copied his actions.

"They'll have guessed we've found the weapons by now. So they'll have to rethink."

"We can hold them off," Clair said, "but we can't get out while they're down there."

Bolan loaded the MP-5 he'd brought along. He cocked it and set the SMG to autofire. He held it out to Clair and ran through the operating procedure, showing her how to eject the empty magazine and reload.

"Hold the trigger down and it fires until you let go. Try not to burn off a full mag in one go. Short bursts are best."

"It sounds as if you're leaving me," she said.

"Only for as long as it takes to check what's on the other side of the end door. Could be a way out." He touched her shoulder. "I need you to make sure they don't sneak up on us. Doesn't matter if you don't hit anything—just so you keep their heads down."

Clair watched him slip two of the magazines under his belt. The rest he left for her use, along with the ammunition box.

"Go," she said.

Bolan went to the end of the passage. He worked the steel bolts. They were relatively new and slid open easily. The heavy latch lifted smoothly. The door was obviously used regularly. Bolan had an idea what he would find on the other side as he pulled the door open.

He heard the hiss of rain, before a slight wind blew it in through the open door. Even in the dim light Bolan could see that this section of the château had a flat roof. In the middle was a large white-painted circle—a helicopter landing pad.

The roof was easily large enough to accommodate a chopper. A convenient way to remove and deliver goods.

Bolan thought back to the two rooms behind him. The château must be the mob's distribution point as well as a meeting place for the combined heads of the conglomerate. They had chosen it well. Fairly isolated, and with the helicopter pad providing a solid means for moving their illicit merchandise. Knowing the financial clout of the mob, there would also likely be some local protection—cover to prevent curious eyes from straying too close to the property.

Bolan scanned the rooftop. A low wall edged the perimeter. He crossed to the closest and peered over. The stone wall would not provide any climbing handholds. He chanced a similar check of the other sides and saw the same. No one was going to scale those near-sheer walls, nor would he and Clair be able to climb down—which was not good news.

Turning, about to go back inside, Bolan raised his eyes and scanned the main bulk of the château. He spotted cast-iron downpipes fixed to the wall next to the door he had exited. He followed the line of the pipe. It terminated in guttering fifteen feet up. Bolan studied it. A chancy offering, but at least a possibility. He stood in front of the downpipe and gripped it—it felt firm, anchored to the stone wall with metal brackets.

He went back inside, closing and bolting the door, his mind figuring the odds. They had to be marginally better than staying inside the building if they took to the château roof.

Clair glanced at him as he rejoined her. She touched his wet face. "Nice night?"

"Any activity down there?"

"Nothing I can see. But I can hear them moving around."

"We need to get out of here," Bolan said. "I found a way. Not the best, but it's all we're likely to get."

"Okay," she said slowly. "Am I going to like this?"

Bolan managed a smile. "I doubt it. How are you with heights?"

"I like riding on tall horses. Sorry, Ethan always says I have a perverse sense of humor."

"There's a way we can get onto the main roof. From there we can find a way to ground level."

"Then we should take it, Matt. Those people are not going to let us walk out of the front door, so we'll have to make our own exit."

"There's a secondary reason we need to go now. We have to get out of here before Corrigan calls in backup."

While Bolan stayed watching the stairs he sent Clair to collect a couple more MP-5s. They filled a few more magazines and loaded the extra weapons. They strapped the SMGs across their backs and carried as many filled magazines as they could.

"Matt," Clair said, "can we go before I chicken out?"

A soft sound from below alerted Bolan to the possibility of another assault.

"Go and unbolt that door," he said.

He waited until Clair freed the door. He took one of the loaded MP-5 guns and fired off steady bursts at the shadowed lower landing. When the H&K was empty, Bolan put it down. As he moved along the passage he paused at the room where the ordnance was stored. Inside the room he opened the box holding the M-67 grenades and pulled four out, slipping them into the large pockets of his blacksuit, then joined Clair.

"Ladies first," he said, showing her the downpipe.

She swung her MP-5 across her shoulders, grasped the pipe and began climbing. The rain made the pipe slippery but she braced her feet against the wall and pulled herself up. Bolan let her reach the halfway mark before he started up.

"A girl could never complain about a date with you being boring," Bolan heard her say.

She reached the top of the pipe and paused briefly to catch her breath.

"There's a walkway round the edge," Clair said as she hauled herself over the parapet.

Bolan saw her shadowy form roll over the low wall and drop out of sight. He dug in, muscles pushing him up and he grasped the gritty stone parapet, pulling himself over the ledge. He slid down next to Clair.

"No sweat," she said.

Bolan looked around. The sloping roof rose behind them, the slates glistening in the fading light. Mossy growths spread out from the edges.

"That way," Bolan said. "Toward the rear of the building."

He had spotted a narrow walkway between the two main angles of the roof—access for workers having to take care of repairs.

A muted shout came from below.

"They know we're up here," Clair said.

"Let's go."

They stepped across the slippery roof slates until they were able to reach the walkway. There were wooden slats to tread on. They were rotten and creaked with every step, some of the slats splitting underfoot.

Bolan brought up the rear. He had a feeling Corrigan's shooters would show themselves sooner rather than later. And he heard rising voices behind him almost as the thought formed in his mind.

He turned, crouching, and saw the head and shoulders of an eager pursuer. The man was dragging himself over the wall, the gleam of his SMG in his right hand. Bolan shouldered the MP-5, lined up his target and eased back on the trigger. The 9 mm burst hit the man in his upper chest. He uttered a startled scream as the impact of the slugs pushed him away from the wall and he vanished from Bolan's sight. Excited shouting followed in the wake of the body's impact on the roof below.

Bolan caught up with Clair. He saw where the walkway angled to the left, cutting across the width of the château.

"Take that direction," he called.

She turned abruptly, without question. Bolan heard her grumble as rotten slats of wood snapped underfoot and she stumbled. She swore forcibly.

"Such language from a young lady," he said.

"My dates don't usually end up with me being chased across rooftops in the rain," she said. "I think I'm excused."

She froze, peering through the gloom ahead.

Bolan had picked up on the sound, too.

"Down," he yelled.

Clair dropped to her stomach and Bolan saw a pair of figures separate ahead of them, weapons starting to rise.

Bolan didn't have time to take evasive action. He centered the MP-5 and fired out of instinct, the flame from the muzzle brightening the shadows. His bursts found their targets. Bodies jerked under the tearing impact, twisting in shock. One toppled to the side, crashing hard on the sloping roof. Slates cracked and dislodged. The other man went flat on his back, his own weapon firing harmlessly skyward.

"Clair?" Bolan called as he moved up to where she was already scrambling to her feet.

"I'm fine. A lot dirtier than when I fell, but okay."

"They've got other ways to reach the roof," Bolan said. "Not so good for us."

"Well thanks for that cheery information."

"Let's keep moving." Bolan had something else to tell her and realized there was no easy way to do it. "If anything moves and it's not me, shoot. Don't think about it. Just shoot."

They moved off again, cutting along the walkway, feeling the rain-soaked wood splintering in places underfoot. The dusk seemed to be hanging around, full dark making no attempt to drop. It allowed them to see their way ahead—but the same would apply to Corrigan's men.

A flutter of movement came from their left—the bulk of an armed man raising over the angle of a slated rise. Clair saw the man a fraction of a second before Bolan. The MP-5 in her hands swung around and she triggered a rising burst that ripped and splintered roof slates. The would-be shooter threw up an arm to deflect the flying slate splinters and that distraction allowed Bolan the time to track and fire himself. The man shuddered under the impact of the American's 9 mm slugs, tumbling back out of sight.

Raised voices warned them of more opposition. They heard the scrape and clatter as heavy boots dislodged slates. Bolan heard a splintering crash followed by a startled yell. It sounded as if someone had broken through a section of the roof. When he rounded the next angle of the walkway, Bolan saw a trio gathered round a fourth man who had half fallen through a section of roof.

One of the men lifted his head as Bolan appeared and screamed a warning to his buddies. As one, they let go of their companion, snatching at the SMGs dangling from shoulder straps.

Bolan crouched forward, his MP-5 settling on the trio, finger easing back on the trigger. The H&K thundered out a scything burst that hit the three men in a moment of terrible savagery. The 9 mm slugs punched in, tearing at flesh and bone, spinning the bloodied figures apart. Bolan hit hard and fast, making sure none of them would be capable of rising again.

The fourth shooter, his scraped raw fingers trying for a grip on the wet, slippery slates, stared at Bolan. His face was speckled with blood from his dead teammates. For a moment he locked eyes with Bolan, a silent plea for help showing. Bolan made no immediate move to assist him as he ejected the MP-5's empty magazine and snapped in a fresh one. Wood and slate cracked beneath the wriggling guy's weight. He felt himself going and let out a hard scream. Then he was gone, trailing debris and dust in his wake. His long scream lasted until he made contact far below.

As they edged by the downed trio, Bolan noticed they were loaded with extra weapons.

"They must be really serious about stopping us," Clair observed.

"You think?"

They hurried forward, eager to reach the far side of the château. The rain fell harder, bouncing off the slated roof and streaming down to hinder them as they splashed through the pooling water.

Bolan threw out a restraining hand, drawing Clair close and easing her into shadow. Ahead he could see the low wall that marked the edge of the roof. A lone figure was standing guard over the iron rail of a ladder fixed to the château wall. He was hunched over against the rain, the collar of a glistening coat turned up around his ears. Bolan was unable to make out his features but he suspected the man would not be wearing a pleased expression at having drawn this solitary position.

The man turned away, staring out from the edge of the roof as he lowered his head to light the cigarette gripped between his lips. Bolan saw the flare of a lighter. The man's SMG was dangling by its strap as he used both hands in his attempt to light his cigarette.

Bolan saw his chance and took it.

He sprinted forward, muscles powering him ahead, closing the gap in seconds. The man's head came up at the last moment and he turned, eyes suddenly wide with alarm. The cigarette clung to his lower lip as he began to yell. Hands dropped to the SMG. Bolan's left shoulder hit him chest high and the man went back off the edge of the roof, arms windmilling frantically. He gave a brief scream as he fell. The thud of his body hitting the ground ended any sound he was making.

"Come on," Bolan shouted.

Clair joined him. She peered over the edge of the roof at the narrow metal ladder.

"Down *that?*"

"Or jump," Bolan said. He grasped the metal rail and swung his legs over the low wall. He took a few steps down. The rungs felt solid enough. "Stay close," he said.

With Clair just above him, Bolan led the way down the ladder. The rail was cold and wet. The rain persisted, soaking through his clothing. If anything, it confirmed he was still alive.

Ten feet left.

Bolan heard the crunch of boots on the gravel below.

He let himself slide the next few feet, ready to let go of the ladder.

The sounds came closer.

Someone shouted in French. Bolan knew enough of the language to understand the challenge.

He let go of the ladder, tensing himself for the drop. He grasped the MP-5 and felt the impact as he struck the ground, rolling forward and came up facing the two armed shooters as they emerged out of the gloom.

"Merde."

Still half-crouched, Bolan opened up, stitching the pair with 9 mm death. His concentrated fire drove them off their feet.

Clair was at his side then, gripping his arm, breathing hard. Her fingers clutched at his him. She was doing her best to hold it together.

"Front of the house," Bolan said. "We'll try for a vehicle."

"Sounds good," she said. "Make it a very fast one."

Staying close to the wall they worked their way toward the front of the château. Peering around the edge of the stone wall Bolan saw the collection of vehicles parked near the front entrance.

Light spilled out from the overwhelming percentage of windows, casting illumination across the frontage. He saw armed figures spill out from the wide-open front doors. Beside him Clair drew in a sharp breath.

"They still seem upset about something," she said.

"Losing their ticket to the big prize gets people that way," Bolan said.

"Now I'm a ticket. First prize, I hope."

Bolan spent a few seconds assessing the situation. There

was little chance of them reaching one of the parked cars without being seen. And he hadn't quite finished with the mob yet.

"I want you to do something for me, Clair," he said. "No argument. Just do what I ask."

The tone of his voice told her this was beyond the time for making light remarks.

"Tell me."

Bolan pointed away from the house in the direction of the dark area beyond the spill of lights. There was thick undergrowth and close-standing trees.

"Cut around to the left, away from our position. Straight into the bushes. Find a place where you can hide yourself. Flat on the ground. Watch the house. Stay where you are until I come to fetch you. Go now."

Clutching the SMG to her chest Clair moved away from him, making no comment as she faded into the darkness. Out of sight and sound. She followed his commands because she realized what he had to do required his full attention. He did not need her close to him, where he would have had to look out for her safety. This time his strike would bring matters to an end and she knew he had to focus fully.

The château was about to become his killing ground.

The Executioner was setting himself up for the end battle in his campaign to bring down the mob.

The ruling heads of the organized crime mob were about to face abdication. Their reign of violence and savagery, corruption and coercion, was coming to a close. Through their actions they had denied themselves any plea for mercy. In the lead up to this night, money and power, the brushing aside of any veneer of humanity had condemned them.

I am not their judge.

I am not their jury.

I am their Executioner.

27

Bolan skirted the spread of light, merging with the darkness, and circled around until he was concealed by the parked cars. The rain was slanting in hard, driving across the château grounds in shimmering waves. But Bolan was beyond even feeling it, his focus on what lay in front of him. From where he crouched he could see through the wide set of windows to the right of the main entrance. That was the room where Corrigan had taken him, presenting his captive to the mob bosses. He could see them, still gathered around the long table. There looked to be a great deal of heated conversation taking place.

They still seem upset about something, Clair had said.

Her words hit the spot.

That *something* was Bolan. He had disrupted their plans. Taken away the advantage they had gained by kidnapping Sorin's sister. And on top if that, he had taken on their hired muscle and created chaos.

A cold smile etched itself across Bolan's bruised and battered face, stinging the tender flesh.

It was payback time.

So you like pain?

You like to see suffering?

Then sit back and watch this night's final performance.

Bolan saw the slow approach of one of the armed shooters. The man was peering back and forth, checking around the parked cars, edging closer to where Bolan crouched, his

SMG allowed to hang from its strap. He didn't want to alert the others until he was closer to the house.

Bolan shrank deeper into the gloom as the heavy tread of the man brought him to the rear of the last car. As the man turned away from him, Bolan stood silently. A dark figure, shedding runnels of rainwater as he rose to his full height, powerful hands reaching out to encircle the unwary sentry, one big hand clamping over the man's mouth to shut off any warning cry. Bolan dragged his prey behind the bulk of the big SUV, tripping him with a leg sweep. Bolan followed the man down, slammed one knee into the lower spine and grasped his head in both hands. The man had no chance to make any sound as Bolan pulled back, twisting hard until the neck and spinal cord separated with a soft grating of bone. He went into spasm and just as quickly became limp.

On his feet, Bolan held the H&K strapped across his chest as he closed on his target—the window of the room where the mob heads were gathered. As he cleared the bunched cars, Bolan saw the second outside man turn in his direction, SMG coming up. The man triggered too soon and the shots burned the air inches away, giving Bolan the opportunity to break his stride and hit the shooter with a controlled burst. The sentry tumbled in an ungainly sprawl.

And Bolan continued his run at the window. Mere feet away he triggered the contents of his magazine at the glass. The window imploded, sending glittering shards into the room. Bolan had a glimpse of startled figures turning, staring at the shattered window.

By this time he had dropped a hand into a deep pocket of his blacksuit, lifting out one of the grenades, pulling the pin and hurling the grenade in through the window. Bolan repeated the action with the other three grenades. Then he was running for the front entrance, having snapped a fresh magazine into the MP-5.

The first grenade detonated as Bolan hit the stone steps, barreling in through the doorway and angling to the left. He heard the detonation, followed by shrill screams. Then the second, third and fourth explosions. The closed doors of the conference room blew out, a cloud of dust and smoke following. Bolan backed across the hall, pressing against the opposite wall. A shower of debris was sprayed across the hall.

A shrieking figure, covered in dust and shedding blood, stumbled out through the door. The man was hugging his left arm, holding it tight against his body. Bolan caught a glimpse of shredded flesh and bone near the shoulder, the limb practically severed from the body. The MP-5 leveled on the figure and Bolan touched the trigger, hitting the man in the chest and punching him off his feet. The man went facedown and Bolan saw that his upper body was a mass of torn flesh where he had been caught by one of the grenade explosions.

Someone started firing blind from the wrecked room, through the clouds of dust and smoke. Bolan heard slugs slam into the wall over his head. He returned fire, moving his muzzle back and forth, high and low. As soon as he had exhausted his magazine, Bolan threw the empty weapon aside and brought the second one he was carrying into operation. The powerful chatter of the SMG filled the dusty hall with its sound. Bolan fired into the room, picking up on anything that moved, or that he imagined was moving. He cleared two full magazines before his finger moved from the trigger and he felt his tension slip away.

The pause that followed was broken only by the occasional sound of debris detaching somewhere in the confines of the silent room. Dust slowly dispersed. Smoke hung close to the ceiling. Bolan heard the patter of rain drifting in through the shattered window.

He reloaded the MP-5—an automatic response to having an empty weapon.

He heard a sound off to his left. It came from the first landing. Bolan moved, stepping away from the wall to clear himself from being spotted. He waited in the alcove created by the main room's door frame.

Someone spoke in French.

Anger.

Confusion.

Bolan let them reach midway down the stairs before he stepped out, the SMG picking out the armed figures as they appeared. The crackle of autofire filled the hallway. Bolan had dropped low, so the opposition's bursts impacted against the edge of the alcove, showering him with stone chips. His accurate return fire caught the two shooters in the open and pitched them back against the stairs. They rolled and jerked as they slithered lifelessly down to the floor.

Bolan turned and stepped into the grenade-blasted room. The multiple explosions had torn the room apart. The long table had splintered down the middle. Chairs had been tossed aside. The wall coverings had been scorched and tattered. Bookshelves hung askew, their contents on the floor.

The deadly effects of the grenades on the human occupants of the room was similarly devastating. The mob heads lay scattered in bloody poses. Shrapnel from the bursting grenades had sliced and ripped into them. Blood was spattered and torn clothing exposed shredded flesh and bone. Bolan's follow-up volleys of 9 mm slugs had found some of the bodies too. No one was moving. The stench of death hung heavily.

"My mistake was not shooting you the minute Ketch brought you off that boat."

Bolan turned and saw Corrigan.

The man was still alive.

But barely.

Slumped against a wall he stared at Bolan through a mask of blood that covered his face and drenched his shirt. A large flap of raw flesh hung from his scalp. Fragments of skull were exposed. The left side of his upper body had been ripped open by a grenade blast, the clothing gone to show the massive wound. A pulped mass of flesh showed splintered ribs. Corrigan was bleeding freely, spitting it from his bloody mouth.

"You had your chance," Bolan said. "Remember what I

said at the beginning. I promised to take your mob apart. Piece by piece. I made you walking dead men. I like to keep my promises."

Corrigan's right hand lifted from his side. He held his pistol, trying to raise it. The effort made him gasp. He dragged his left arm across his body. When Bolan saw it he realized there was no hand left. It had been blown off during the grenade burst. Corrigan's eyes blazed with defiance through the bloody mask covering his face.

"I need to kill you, Cooper, you son of a bitch."

Bolan centered the muzzle of the MP-5, his finger finding the trigger.

"Game over," he said and fired, the long burst virtually demolishing Corrigan's head.

There was a cell phone on the floor near Corrigan, the screen flashing. Bolan picked it up. The message was informing Corrigan a text message was waiting to be opened. Bolan thumbed the button to read the message.

Can't make contact with anyone. What's going on? Need update about Sorin's sister.

Bolan reread the message a couple of times. He pressed Reply and was presented with a screen showing a blank area and a cell phone number at the top. That was all he needed for the moment. He closed the phone down.

Bolan stepped outside, feeling the cold rain on his face. He turned and made his way to where he had sent Clair.

"It's Matt," he called. "You can show yourself now."

"How do I know it's you?" she replied, taunting him even as she merged from the deep undergrowth. "Maybe you're trying to trick me, *Yank*."

"Only Ethan Sorin's sister would say that."

She stood facing him, holding out the MP-5. "Can I get rid of this now?"

Bolan took the SMG from her. He led her toward the parked

cars, choosing the SUV Corrigan had used to bring him to the château. He opened the rear door and placed the weapons on the floor behind the seat, except for one autopistol. As they climbed in, Clair reached down into the foot well and pulled something onto her lap. It was Bolan's holdall.

"Open it up," Bolan said. "Should be a sat phone in there."

Clair searched the contents, handing him the phone. He powered it up, then contacted Stony Man Farm.

"Can you pinpoint my current location?" he asked when Aaron Kurtzman answered.

"Do not insult me with a question like that. I'm sitting in front of millions of dollars' worth of computers and all you want is a location?"

Bolan failed to hold back a grin at Kurtzman's rant. He would work his cyber magic and have Bolan's position without working up a sweat. Kurtzman maintained a nonstop grumble about being underused until he completed the task.

"Coordinates on their way to your phone," he said.

"Thanks," Bolan said. "You can go back to your *Popular Mechanics* magazine now."

The last thing Bolan heard was Kurtzman's booming laughter as he finished the call.

Bolan started the SUV, spun it round and drove away. He took it back along the road in the direction of the coast. Once they were well clear of the château, Bolan called Henning on the sat phone.

"Where the hell have you been?" the Brit asked.

"Long story, Greg. I'm in France. Clair Sorin is sitting beside me. She's unhurt. I'm going to give you coordinates for a château. Get your people to make a visit. You'll find the head honchos of the mob there."

"They liable to put up any kind of resistance?" Henning asked, though his tone suggested he already knew the answer.

"They're in no condition to do anything," Bolan said. "On the top floor of the house you'll find some early Christmas presents in the form of drugs, ordnance and a pile of cold, hard cash. I think the place was used as a regional distribution point."

Henning was silent for a moment. "Sounds as if we'll have to put this down to another intergang fallout."

"One more thing," Bolan said. He opened up the cell he'd found next to Corrigan and read the text message, following it up with the sender's number. "I'm sure you'll make use of that."

"You can count on that, mate. You need any assist getting out of the country?"

"If I do, I'll let you know."

Bolan glanced across at Clair. She had tipped the seat back and was slumped in a relaxed position, already asleep. He didn't wake her until much later. By then he was parked on the quayside where the *Venture* was still moored. The recent storm had kept the vessel from leaving.

He checked his handgun, smiling to himself as he opened his door.

"Isn't that the *Venture?*" Clair asked.

"Bring the holdall and we'll go say hello to the crew."

He reached inside and picked up the MP-5s.

As they walked toward the boat Clair said, "They're in for a surprise."

"Hope it's not too much of a shock," Bolan said. "They're going to take us back across the channel."

"England? Home?" Clair said. "And not a minute too soon, Mr. Cooper."

28

The task-force squad room was half full when Greg Henning walked in. He was followed by his immediate superior, who hung back as Henning crossed to his desk. Standing beside it, he called for attention.

"Couple of announcements I have to make. Ethan's sister has been located. She's on her way home. Ethan has been informed, and he's recovering from his injury. The other thing is the mob headmen have been taken down. They were gathered in France for a heads-up meeting at a château they used as a headquarters. Our European division has been in and verified that none of the bastards survived. They were all dead by the time the team showed up. Looks like someone went in to rescue Clair Sorin and had to use excessive force to pull her out. The team also located a large stash of drugs, weapons and money. So a good result all round."

Henning glanced across the room to where Tony Hanley was sitting behind his desk. The man's face had paled and his eyes were staring straight ahead. Henning looked in the direction of his boss, who nodded for Henning to continue.

"That, Tony, is why your text message received no answer. Because Corrigan was already dead when you sent it."

"I…don't know what you mean…." Hanley protested. He half rose from his seat. By this time every pair of eyes in the room was fixed on him. "You can't…"

"We can, you miserable bastard," Henning said. "You made

it easy for us by texting on your *own* cell this time. Were you panicking because you'd been left out of the loop? Forgot to use your burn phone? Didn't take a lot of effort to track down who owned the number from that text."

There was a rising sound of anger as the team turned on Hanley. He was surrounded by the men he had been betraying, and if their superior had not ordered them back, they might have descended on him.

Henning pushed his way to stand in front of Hanley. He held out a hand. "Give me your weapon," he said. "Empty your pockets on the desk."

Hanley took the autopistol from its holster and handed it over. Henning ejected the magazine and worked the slide to push out the bullet in the chamber. He dropped the pistol on the desk, placing the magazine in his pocket.

He started to turn away. Then without warning he spun back around and brought up his right fist in a powerful swing that slammed against Hanley's jaw, the force knocking the man backward. Hanley clawed at the desk to hold himself up. Blood was already spilling from his mouth down onto his shirt.

"You could have broken my jaw," he yelled.

Henning looked down at his bruised knuckles. "Bloody hell, I must be losing my touch."

"I'll fucking sue you," Hanley shouted as his hands were pulled behind his back and his wrists cuffed, none too gently.

"Why?" somebody said. "Not our fault you tripped and fell."

"That's what I saw."

"Me, too."

Another voice added, "Be careful you don't trip and fall again."

"Quit while you're ahead," Henning's boss said. "You're in enough trouble already. Leaking information. Implicit in the murder of your fellow agents. The kidnapping of Clair Sorin. Accepting money from known criminals. Now we know where to look, we'll get it all, Tony."

"And no mob to help bail you out," Henning said. "You're done."

"Get him out of here," the boss said. "Make sure he's well looked after until it's time to move him on."

Hanley was hustled away, protesting wildly. Henning stood checking out the contents of Hanley's pockets. He picked up the cell and went through it to the Send list. When he located the text Bolan had found on Corrigan's phone, he showed it to his boss.

"He's sent it a half dozen times."

"If we can get hold of the phone belonging to Corrigan it will confirm everything," Henning's boss said.

"I'll get it."

"From your *Yank?*"

Henning only smiled.

"Greg, you sailed pretty close to the wind on this."

"How so, boss?"

"Don't be smart. This American has run riot over the past few days. Broken every rule in the bloody book. I think he may have also invented a few of his own."

"He's achieved what we haven't been able to," Henning said. "And he pulled Ethan and his sister out of trouble. And now we'll have that information Ethan's been hanging on to."

"Does that justify his Wild West tactics?"

"End result is the breakup of the mob. The ruling elite taken down. It'll help us complete the cleanup. Off the record, boss, I'd say it does."

"Seeing as off the record is the flavor of the day, I have to agree, Greg. But next time you talk to your cowboy, remind him we don't want a repeat if he hits the U.K. again."

"I'll do that, sir."

"Oh, what the hell. Tell him thanks, as well."

BOLAN WAS BACK at the hotel he had been booked in originally. Stony Man Farm had called and kept his room available, and he was thankful for that. Clair had been reunited with her brother. Sorin had delivered his files and the OrgCrime force was busy using the information. The mob was in chaos, splitting apart and going for cover. Names were being pursued over their connection to the mob. At this moment, the only people profiting were the lawyers hastily summoned to start earning their high fees.

Passing off his still-apparent bruises as the result of an automobile accident, Bolan had retired to his hotel room for some R and R. He stood under the shower first, then rang Room Service and asked for food and coffee to be delivered. He told Reception he didn't want to be disturbed and hung the notice on his door. After eating his fill, Bolan retired to his bed and gave in to his body's screaming demand for rest.

Apart from the occasional visits from Room Service Bolan saw no one. He had not realized just how tired he was. He stayed in the room for two more days, then decided he needed to return to the land of the living. He ordered a breakfast tray, pulled out fresh clothing from his wardrobe and risked a shave after a shower.

His sat phone, switched off, had been plugged into a power outlet to recharge the battery. When he turned it on, he had close to a dozen messages. He called Stony Man Farm and assured them he was fine, then asked for Brognola. The big Fed told him the phone lines had been buzzing since news about the mob had got around. Anthony "Tony" Lowell's death had set off an internal struggle for power within the New York mob. A number of hits had eliminated other rising stars within the criminal fraternity, and the U.S. OrgCrime unit had been closing in because of the names in the files Sorin had brought in.

"I don't have to tell you how I feel about the dead OrgCrime agents," Brognola said, "but the fallout is making a lot of people happy. Your pal, Ethan, has made it a lot easier to get to the right people. They're scrambling over each other to point the finger and try to make deals. The Justice Department is lending a hand."

"Just make sure none of them wriggle out from under," Bolan said. "Too many good people have died to let anyone walk free."

Brognola was silent for a moment. "If any do, Striker, I can always pass their names along to you."

"Spoken like a true upholder of law and order," Bolan said.

"Damn right."

Later, Bolan spoke to Henning again.

"If they knew where to get hold of you, the boys here would be begging to buy you a drink," Henning told him.

"I might take them up on that," Bolan said.

"How are you doing?"

"Taking it easy."

"Okay for some," Henning said. "Our teams are running around like headless chickens since we took out the mole. Things are coming together nicely. Unofficially, you get our thanks."

"You getting any backlash?"

"Uh-uh. The official word is a mob-related firefight at the château that resulted in a number of criminal deaths."

"A thieves-falling-out kind of thing."

"Exactly. Matt, what you did for Ethan and his sister will not be forgotten."

"He was a good agent—a good man—in trouble. I was glad to help."

"Oh, yeah, by the way," Henning said, "I had a call from a young woman name of Lauren. She asked me to pass along a message. Something along the lines of her being okay and not to worry. And if she ever comes across you again…" Henning paused. "I'm not repeating that part in front of company."

Bolan laughed. He could use his imagination to work that out.

Someone tapped on his door. He made his excuses to Henning and said he would call later. Crossing the room Bolan checked the spy hole to see who was waiting. Then he opened the door.

"Hey," he said.

Clair Sorin stood there. Dressed in a cream trouser suit and a dark shirt, she looked beautiful.

"Mr. Cooper," she said.

"Miss Sorin."

"Am I going to have to stand here all day?"

"No. Would you like to come in?"

"That was almost hard work. And, *yes,* I certainly would like to come in."

It wasn't as if Bolan needed any further persuasion.

* * * * *

TAKE 'EM FREE
2 action-packed novels plus a mystery bonus

NO RISK
NO OBLIGATION TO BUY

ReaderService.com

Manage your account online!

- Review your order history
- Manage your payments
- Update your address

*We've designed
the Harlequin® Reader Service
website just for you.*

Enjoy all the features!

- Reader excerpts from any series
- Respond to mailings and special monthly offers
- Discover new series available to you
- Browse the Bonus Bucks catalog
- Share your feedback

Visit us at:

ReaderService.com